Mystery on
Mackinac Island

MYSTERY ON
MACKINAC ISLAND

Anna W. Hale

Mystery on Mackinac Island ©1989, 1998 by the estate of Anna Hale
Illustrations ©1989, 1998 by Lois McLane
First Thunder Bay Press edition published 1998

Printed in the United States of America

05 04 03 02 01 00   6   5   4   3   2

ISBN 1-882376-48-X

Library of Congress Cataloging-in-Publication Data

Hale, Anna. 1909–1998
Mystery on Mackinac Island / by Anna Hale;
illustrations by Lois McLane
p. cm.
Summary: Thirteen-year-old Hunter Martineau, an Ottawa
Indian, and his tourist friends, Rusty and Jancy, investigate
the mystery of stolen bicycles on Mackinac Island.
ISBN 1-882376-48-X: $10.95
[1. Mystery and detective stories. 2. Ottawa Indians – Fiction.
3. Indians of North America – Fiction.
4. Mackinac Island (Mich.) – Fiction.]
I. McLane, Lois. 1953 – ill.   II. Title.
PZ7.H1288My   1989 [Fic] – dc20   89-35484

Holt, Michigan

AUTHOR'S NOTE

The island setting in this story is accurate, but all the characters are imaginary, with the exception of Chief Walking Buffalo of Alberta, Canada. He visited Mackinac several times, and might well have had such an encounter as is depicted in the book.

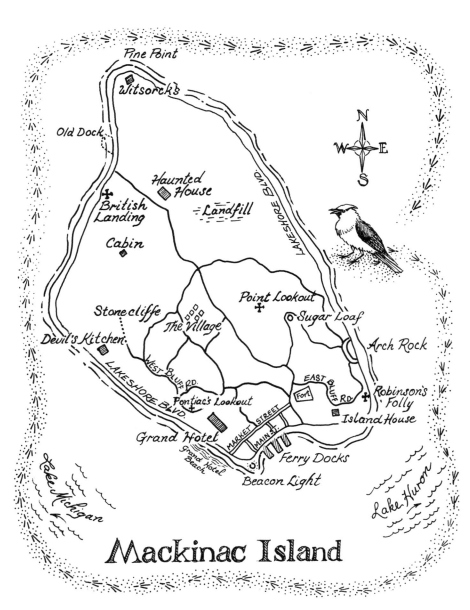

Mackinac Island

CONTENTS

THE BICYCLE MYSTERY

When thirteen-year-old Hunter heard that bicycles were being stolen day after day on the island where he lived, he couldn't have cared less. He had enough problems already.

For years the Indian boy had lived with his grandfather, deep in the woods of Mackinac, but now the "Old Chief" was dead, and Hunter's special world of woods and wildlife was crashing around him.

As the teenager and his father walked away from the pine-shaded cemetery on Mackinac Island, in Michigan, Tim said,

"It's okay, son. You can live in the village, with Bella and the kids and me."

"I don't want to!" Hunter said. "I want to stay in the cabin."

"That's impossible," his father answered. "I can't give you any money, and Grandfather's pension has stopped."

"I'll work," Hunter said. "There's lots of jobs in the tourist season."

"You can't get a work permit. You're too young."

"I'll find work!" Hunter insisted. "And live where I want to."

At last, after more arguing, Tim gave in. "Okay. Try it for the summer. But when school starts, you move in with us. That's final."

Tim turned toward the village, calling out, "Be sure to lock your bike! If it gets stolen, you're out of luck."

Hunter headed for the cabin, glowing with a sense of victory. The rest of the summer was his!

That afternoon Hunter rode his bicycle toward the harbor to look for work. As he passed Old Fort Mackinac on the bluff above the City of Mackinac Island he saw tourist bikes left outside the walls, and remembered his father's warning. Well, he always locked his bike. It would never be stolen.

When he had coasted down the hill to Main Street, and had parked his bike behind the library, he went in to tell Mrs. Purcell about needing a job. She had been his friend since he had learned to read. She might help.

The small, gray-haired librarian listened thoughtfully as Hunter explained the situation.

"If I hear of a job," she said, "I'll put the cedar waxwing in the front window as a signal. When you see it there, come in."

Hunter grinned. He had found that little bird, dead, outside the library window when he was only nine. Because he had felt so bad about its being killed, Mrs. Purcell had it mounted, and kept it on her desk. Today he marveled again at its beauty and exquisite colors. It gave him hope.

Still there were butterflies in his stomach as he went into the Chippewa Hotel, nearest to the ferry docks. It seemed terribly dark in there, and he felt as if the walls were closing in on him. With a dry mouth he asked the woman behind the desk about a job. She waved him to another door that was partly open. Inside was a man with a moustache, who was working at a littered desk.

Looking up, he said in an annoyed voice, "What do you want?"

"A job," Hunter said.

"Any experience?"

Hunter shook his head.

"How old are you?"

"Thirteen," Hunter answered.

"Sorry. You can't get a work permit until you're sixteen."

Hunter went out, almost glad to be turned down. He couldn't imagine working in a building like that, and with strangers who came to the island only to make money. They didn't love Mackinac as he did.

Out in the sunshine again, he felt better. Crowds of tourists were milling around on the sidewalks, and in the street horse-drawn carriages big and small were on the move. Dozens of cyclists on rented bikes were trying to make their way through the traffic.

There were no cars. On Mackinac Island the only motorized vehicles were the doctor's station wagon and the fire engine.

Hunter crossed the street to the Murray Hotel, hoping for better luck. It was not as dark as the Chippewa, and the manager was more friendly, but Hunter was told again, "We can't hire a thirteen-year-old."

That was what he heard everywhere he went, in hotels and boarding houses up and down Main and Market Streets. Hunter was tall and strong for his age. He thought he could make people believe he was sixteen, but his grandfather had told him again and again, "Never speak with a forked tongue." He couldn't bring himself to tell that lie.

He tried the souvenir and specialty stores, and the

shops where the famous Mackinac Fudge was made and sold. No luck anywhere. By this time all Hunter wanted was to go home.

Home! As he thought of that snug cabin tucked away in the dense woods, he knew he just *had* to live there. It would be lonely, but at least he would be living close to the wild animals and birds as he and his grandfather had always done. In Harrisonville with the family he would have no chance for bird study. So he had to earn money. Where should he look next?

At the far end of Main Street was the Beacon Light Hotel. Its manager was an island man, not a stranger. Maybe he could help, but the boy's hopes were low as he pushed his way through the crowd of tourists in that direction.

This hotel, painted white with green trim, was more like an over-sized summer cottage than a hotel. It faced the lake and had wide, welcoming porches above a green lawn. Mr. French, the manager, a slight, brown-haired man, was standing at the door. He greeted Hunter warmly.

"I'm sorry about your grandfather," he said. "With the Old Chief gone, Mackinac won't be the same. He was a link with the past."

A sudden lump in Hunter's throat kept him from speaking. The man's eyes searched his face.

"Can I do something for you?" he asked.

Swallowing the lump, Hunter said, "I need work. I need it bad."

Mr. French cocked one eyebrow. "Your Dad hasn't lost his job again, I hope?"

"Oh, no," came the answer. "I've got to earn money so I can stay in our cabin. I don't want to live with Dad and Bella and the kids."

Surprised, Mr. French asked, "Why not? They're your family."

"I know," Hunter mumbled, dropping his eyes. "But I tried it once. Bella made fun of me, and her girls got in my hair. I went back to Grandfather."

"Hmm, I see," Mr. French said slowly. "And now with the new baby, their house is more crowded than ever?"

Hunter nodded.

"Well," the manager went on. "Come back in a couple of days. You can mow the lawn, and I'll save some other jobs for you."

"Gee! Thanks, Mr. French. I'll be here Saturday," Hunter promised, turning to go.

"Wait," Mr. French exclaimed, his face lighting up. "I just thought of something better! This afternoon the owners of the Bike Rental shops announced a reward of fifty dollars for anyone who can find the stolen bikes, and another fifty for the arrest of the thief. Why don't you try that?"

Excitement zipped through Hunter. Grandfather had taught him how to track animals to their holes and he could use those same skills to stalk the bicycle thief to his den. It would be fun, and he would get a hundred bucks for doing it!

"How about it?" Mr. French asked.

"You bet! It ought to be a breeze."

"Don't be too sure," Mr. French warned him. "This man is smart. He has already picked up more than a dozen bikes, without leaving a trace."

"It's not smart to steal rental bikes," Hunter answered. "They can be identified easy, with their ID numbers and license tags."

"Humph!" Mr. French responded. "He can yank off the tags, and paint out the ID numbers. But how does he snatch the bikes without being seen? Where does he store them until he can take them off the island to sell?"

"I don't know," Hunter admitted slowly. "but I'm going to find out. I know what I'll do. I'll get all the details I can from the rental shops, and then I'll lay my plan of action."

After a quick goodbye to Mr. French, Hunter went with wings on his feet to the shop of his old friend

Emmet on Market Street. Emmet was an islander. Hunter found him crouching down putting a new tire on a bicycle. His weather-beaten face creased into a smile.

"Hi, Emmet," Hunter said. "Say — have any of your bikes been stolen?"

The friendly smile gave way to a scowl.

"You better believe it," he growled. "Four."

"Well," Hunter said. "I want to have a shot at finding them. Will you help me?"

As he spoke he drew out of his jeans pocket a pencil and notebook he used for bird study. He began asking questions and writing down Emmet's answers, making notes of the ID and license numbers and colors of Emmet's missing bikes. Also when and where they had disappeared. Two had been taken near Sugar Loaf, one outside the Fort, and one below Arch Rock. The story was always the same. The tourist had left the bike just for a minute, but when he turned around again the bike was gone.

From Emmet's it was only a short walk to Mr. Piperman's shop on Main Street. There Hunter got details of more losses. The more he heard, the more excited he got about trying to outwit the bicycle thief.

The two hotels that rented bikes were farther away, so he hurried to the library for his bike. As he unlocked it he decided he ought to tell Mrs. Purcell how he was going to earn a lot of money, but tomorrow would be soon enough.

Hunter rode east on Lakeshore Boulevard, past Marquette Park and the Fort above it, to Island House. After making notes of their losses he went back through town to the Grand Hotel which faced the western shore. It was very big and white and impressive. Hunter was glad the Bike Rental Shop was tucked away in the back. There he filled more pages in his notebook. Then he started for home.

He rode through the village but did not stop to see his Dad. He was too busy trying to work things out in his mind.

Why were rented bikes stolen, but no private bikes? Was the thief an island man who didn't want — or dare — to steal from people he knew? But an islander seen riding a rented bike would be spotted by people who knew him. No, the thief must be a stranger, acting like a tourist. He could ride a stolen bike to his hideout without being noticed. So how would Hunter spot him? There was no easy answer to that question.

After riding through the center of the island, Hunter reached a spot where, on the right, the trees gave way to a grassy area. There was an historic marker about "The Battlefield of 1814." Nearby was an ancient, empty house where soldiers wounded in the battle between Americans and British had been cared for.

Opposite the house was an inconspicuous narrow trail that led through the woods to the Old Chief's home. The two-room cabin was very old, built of well-chinked logs and covered with board siding that had weathered to a soft gray.

Hunter leaned his bike against the small porch, thinking that this house was his ticket to the outdoor life he loved. He put his key in the lock and then hesitated. It was hard to go in knowing that Grandfather was not waiting there, with his wisdom, his special kind of humor, and his unspoken but warm love.

Well, Hunter decided, opening the door, better to be here, alone, than in Dad's noisy house in the village. If he found the stolen bicycles quickly he would have the rest of the summer for birdwatching. If he caught the thief too, maybe he could persuade his Dad he was smart enough to look after himself even when school started.

THOSE BINOCULARS

Under the tall trees Grandfather's cabin seemed dark when Hunter entered. After lighting a kerosene lamp he made a quick fire in the woodstove and soon had a hamburger sizzling there. He got out a bag of chips and had just finished eating his supper when there were footsteps on the porch and a knock on the door. Thinking it must be his Dad he opened the door.

Instead of his father's short, stocky figure he saw the tall muscular shape of Kirby Tyson, the island trash collector. He lived next door to Dad in the village, and Hunter's heart skipped a beat. Was something wrong with Dad?

"Hi, Hunter," the man said. "I couldn't get to the cemetery this morning, but I'm sorry about your grandpa. I wanted to see if there's any way I can help you."

"Thanks," the boy answered. "I'm okay."

Kirby stepped in and looked around. "You got a nice place here," he said. "But I bet you'll be glad to move."

"I'm not moving," Hunter told him.

Kirby looked surprised. "Why not?" he asked. As Hunter was slow in answering, he added, "I bet you didn't know how to get your furniture and stuff to the village. I can give you a hand. We can use the trash wagon, and get most of it in one load. It's waiting now, at the end of your trail!"

"Thanks," Hunter repeated. "but I'm going to get a job and take care of myself, here, until school."

"I'm sorry to hear that," Kirby answered. "Your Dad told me he was hoping you can earn some money and help the family. His work at the stables stops, you know, after Labor Day."

"I know," Hunter mumbled. "but he said I could try this."

Kirby was silent a minute as his eyes wandered around the room. He noticed an owl headdress hanging on the wall, and other items of Indian handcraft on a shelf.

"Have you thought," he questioned, "that if you are away all day working, someone could break in and steal these things?"

"Who would do that?" Hunter asked, upset at the idea of the treasures being stolen.

"Tourists, or teenagers, looking for free souvenirs," Kirby answered. "If they were in your Dad's house they'd be safe."

"Yeah, safe from thieves," Hunter agreed. "But Bella's kids would wreck them in a week."

Again Kirby was quiet, thinking. At last he said, "Face it, Hunter. At your age all you can get is odd jobs. Even those are hard to find. But sometimes when I'm collecting trash people ask me if I know anyone who could do jobs for them. I'd let *you* know, but I can't if you're way out here. Next door to me, in your Dad's house, I could help you pick up some extra bucks."

Hunter shook his head slowly. "Thanks," he muttered, "but I want to stay here."

"That's too bad," Kirby responded. "I really wanted to help you get back to civilization."

"But you see," Hunter explained soberly. "I don't like that civilization."

"Okay, okay," Kirby said, moving toward the door. "But when you change your mind, I'll be glad to move you — for free!"

When Kirby had disappeared down the trail, Hunter's feelings were mixed. It was good of Dad's neighbor to want to help, but the teenager could not bear the thought of living in the village. Today he had learned how hard it would be to earn money, even just for food, but he was going to give it a shot. Thinking of food, he realized he was still hungry. He looked for a piece of fruit. There was none. In fact there was little food of any kind left. Tomorrow he would have to buy more. He would use whatever was left of Grandfather's money.

Opening the drawer where money was kept, he felt around. His fingers came up empty. Then he remembered. He had used the last five-dollar bill to buy medicine for Grandfather. What should he do now? He couldn't ask his father. His teacher, Mr. Clemson, was always ready to help kids, but Hunter didn't feel like asking him. Loneliness swept over the boy. The longing for his grandfather was a sharp thorn in his chest.

The old man's worn moccasins were on the floor by his sturdy wooden chair. After a moment's thought Hunter sat in that chair for the first time in his life. He kicked off his loafers and slid his feet into those moccasins. It gave him a sense of oneness with Grandfather, to wear his shoes and sit in his chair. Maybe if he sat there quietly some of Grandfather's wisdom would flow through . . .

Hunter was keen to lay plans for tracking the bicycle thief, but first he had to earn money for food. After a while an idea came to him. In the morning he would go to the West Bluff and ask for work at the big houses of summer residents. As soon as he had laid in some food, he would get on with the mystery of the disappearing bicycles.

The first step in that project, he decided , would be to stake out Sugar Loaf. More bikes had vanished there than anywhere else, and bushes gave good cover where he could hide. When tourists left their rented bikes to climb around the unusual rock formation, Hunter would be watching to see if the thief came along and rode off on one of them. Hunter would follow at a distance and see where he hid the bike. His last thought before falling asleep was how surprised his Dad would be when Hunter showed him the fifty bucks! Maybe even a hundred!

The next morning Hunter was up with the sun, too early to ask for work but perfect for watching birds. He went to an old cedar tree near the house and drew from a leaf-filled hole at its base a plastic sack containing a pair of powerful binoculars. Putting the strap around his neck he was off through the woods, lost in his own special world.

Two hours later he returned, with more facts in his notebook about the call of the Redstart warbler. As he kneeled by the cedar tree it struck him that there was no need now to hide the binocs. Grandfather was not here to ask where he got them. He took the glasses into the cabin and put them in the knapsack he would carry downtown.

On the West Bluff road Hunter went from house to house where summer residents were living. He offered to mow the lawn, work in the garden, make repairs, or paint. He would cut and haul wood. But today no one wanted his help. It was discouraging.

By the time the sun was high overhead, Hunter knew there was only one thing left to try. He would have to go to the ferry docks and pick up a few quarters by carrying bags for passengers. He shrank from that because it meant talking to tourists, those strange people the islanders called "Fudgies" because they ate so much of the famous Mackinac Fudge.

Before tackling that unpleasant job Hunter took a break, by going out onto the rocky bluff called Pontiac's Lookout. Far below, the lake was sparkling blue and gold in the sunshine. In the distance stretched the miracle bridge, "Mighty Mac", spanning miles of lake from Mackinaw City in the south to St. Ignace on Michigan's northern peninsula. At first the sky was empty. Then he saw a tiny speck in the blueness to the south. Quickly he pulled out the glasses and focused them, hoping he had spotted an eagle. No luck. It was only an airplane heading for the Petoskey airport.

Looking closer to the island-shore he saw a ferry from St. Ignace chugging along, followed by a ballet of gulls. He watched them through the glasses, enjoying their grace and skill. They never even touched each other as they whirled and swirled around the moving boat.

He looked at the passengers. They seemed close enough to touch. He saw a red-haired boy of 12 or 13 standing on the deck looking at the island through binoculars. Hunter studied him. A typical mainland kid. Blue denim shorts, a yellow tee shirt with a cartoon figure on it. Very white skin, and freckles. With a jolt the island boy suddenly realized that the tourist boy's glasses were trained on *him*. The redhead gave a friendly wave and Hunter raised his arm in the salute he used to give Grandfather. Instantly he dropped down out of sight behind a low bush, angry with himself. What did he think he was doing . . . signaling friendship to an unknown Fudgie kid?

When the ferry was out of sight he rode down the hill, parked his bike behind the library and checked the window. No cedar waxwing. Good. He'd see Mrs. Purcell later. First there were those quarters he needed desperately to earn.

He reached the nearest dock just as passengers from Mackinaw City were pushing their way ashore. The St. Ignace boat was unloading at a farther dock.

Among the casually clad, gum-chewing strangers Hunter saw a woman dressed in a creamy white pantsuit. Her silvery hair was in perfect order, and her eyes searched the dock anxiously. She spoke to a girl who was standing by a pile of matched luggage, and then walked up the ramp to the dock. She glanced around uncertainly. Hunter thought that if he could help her she might pay well. As he stepped in front of her she almost bumped into him.

"Well!" she exclaimed. "Can't you look where you're going?"

"I'm sorry," Hunter said. "But can I help you?"

The lady looked down her nose at him. "How can I get to the East Bluff with my luggage?"

"Shall I get you a taxi?" he asked.

The woman's blue-gray eyes opened wide. "A taxi? Oh, yes! I understood the only cars on the island were emergency vehicles."

"There are plenty of taxis," Hunter assured her. "I'll carry your bags to the street and get one for you."

The tall girl left to guard the suitcases looked friendly, with light brown hair fluffy around her face. Hunter thought she might be his age until she grinned at him, showing metal bands on her teeth. She was younger than he — 11 or 12.

He picked up the bags, surprised because some of them seemed almost empty. Leading the way to the street, he signaled to the taxi stand. As the brightly painted horse-drawn surrey pulled up in front of them the lady's mouth dropped open.

"*This* is a taxi?" she gasped.

Keeping his face straight, Hunter pointed to the sign TAXI on the roof. The driver was an old man, and he was having trouble with his bony, restless horses. He told Hunter to pile the bags in the rack behind the seats. The girl climbed in, followed by the woman, who turned and opened her purse. She hesitated, and Hunter was afraid she was going to ask, "How much?" Instead she snapped the purse shut and said,

"You had better come along with us to carry things into the house."

When Hunter had seated himself beside the driver the woman asked, "Driver, do you know where Cragmore House is?"

"Yes ma'am," he answered as he clucked to the horses. "On the East Bluff. Yellow house with a red door. Nobody's been there for years. It's good you're moving in."

With a slight sniff she told him the house had been sold, and she had come to take out the personal things. So, Hunter thought, that explains the empty suitcases. He shifted on the seat so he could study the passengers out of the corner of his eye. Everything he could learn about the island visitors might help him in tracking the thief.

As the horses clip-clopped past Marquette Park the girl looked up with great interest at the historic Fort on the sheer cliff above.

"Aunt Myra," she said. "I've simply got to sketch the Fort while I'm here, and all the other places. I wish we were staying longer."

Her aunt answered, "You'll have plenty of time, Jancy. We'll work every morning, sorting and packing things. Then after lunch while I rest you can see the sights and sketch whatever you like."

After passing the Island House the taxi turned up the steep zigzag road to the bluff. Jancy was twisting her neck like an owl, trying to take in everything at once. (Hunter made a mental note of this. The bicycle thief, though dressed like a tourist, would not be interested in the sights.)

At Cragmore House when the taxi had gone and the bags were inside, the girl turned to Hunter.

"My name is Jancy Southgate," she said. "What's yours? Do you live here on Mackinac Island?"

Hunter noticed that she said "Mackinaw", instead of the harsh "Mackinack" like most strangers.

"Yep," he answered. "My name is Hunter Martineau. How come you know the right way to pronounce 'Mackinac'?"

Jancy explained that this house had belonged to someone in their family a long time, so she had heard a lot about the island. Her aunt, Mrs. DuPont, had inherited the house, and had sold it.

Mrs. DuPont called Hunter to bring the bags upstairs. Then she paid him, quite generously. As he went out the door Jancy followed him.

"What are the most interesting things to see on the island?" she asked. "I'm a history nut, and I like to see unusual things."

"First buy a guidebook at the tourist booth downtown," Hunter suggested. "And then rent a bicycle from Emmet's Shop on Market Street. Then you can see whatever you like."

"Will do!" she said. "How big is the island?"

"About nine miles around, on the lakeshore road," he told her. "Just a nice ride."

As he spoke she had been glancing across the narrow strip of water toward Round Island.

"What's that funny-looking building over there?" she asked.

"That's an abandoned lighthouse."

"How exciting!" she exclaimed. "I wish I could go over there and get a better look at it."

"You'd have to rent a boat," Hunter said. "But I can give you a closer look." He reached into his knapsack and handed her the binoculars. She thanked him and focused them on the old lighthouse.

"Oooh! It's spooky!" she said. "I want to draw that too. What super binoculars!"

Hunter nodded, grinning at her. She wasn't bad for a Fudgie kid. Then she asked, "Where did you get them? They must have cost a fortune!"

Hunter felt himself flush. He couldn't tell her the truth. He hedged.

"They . . . they belonged to a friend," he said. "I'm . . . using them this summer."

"You're lucky!" she said. "What do *you* use them for?"

Hunter was uncomfortable, eager to get away, but he answered. "For birds. I'd like to be a bird man."

"That's great!" Jancy responded. "Maybe some day you'll work with the National Geographic."

Hunter knew that was impossible for a guy like him, but it gave him a lift.

"So long," he said as he started back toward town. To himself he added, "That was a close call. I mustn't let anyone see the binocs."

RUSTY

When he had eaten at a fast-food place down town there wasn't much of Mrs. DuPont's money left and Hunter headed again for the docks. Glancing at the library as he went by, he stopped in his tracks. The cedar waxwing was in the window. Oh, no! That meant Mrs. Purcell had found a job for him. He didn't want a job now, but he had to go in.

"Hunter!" Mrs. Purcell greeted him with excitement. "I've got a great job for you. Only for a week but it pays five dollars a day!"

Hunter didn't answer, torn between needing that kind of money and not wanting to give up the bicycle mystery. By the end of a week someone else might have solved it.

Mrs. Purcell told him she had a phone call from a Mr. Hammergren, who had just arrived for a business conference at the Grand Hotel. He had brought his son along and they were staying at the Beacon Light. The boy was eager to see the island and learn all about the Indians and fur traders. Mr. Hammergren had asked the librarian if she could recommend a young man to show Scott around.

"I told him I had just the right guide for his son, and that you would come to the Beacon Light as soon as I could reach you."

Hunter groaned. This would wreck everything, he thought.

"What's the matter?" Mrs. Purcell asked.

Hunter protested. "I don't know how to tell a mainland kid about the island."

The librarian smiled. "Once you get started," she promised, "you won't have any trouble, because the island is close to your heart."

Then Hunter had to tell her about wanting to use all his time for solving the bicycle mystery.

"But that's perfect!" she cried. "While you show Scott around, the two of you can do the detective job together!"

Hunter didn't think it would work, but at last she persuaded him to give it a try.

Wheeling his bike, Hunter made his way slowly down the street. As he went up the path to the Beacon Light Hotel a red-haired boy in blue shorts came bounding down the steps, his arms flung wide as though he were flying. He skidded to a stop in front of the island youth, his round blue eyes staring.

"Are you Hunter Martineau? he asked breathlessly.

At the same instant both boys realized they had seen each other this morning. Through their binoculars. Hunter's impulse was to get away, but his feet seemed rooted to the ground. He nodded.

"It's you!" the red head whooped. "Man-oh-man, what luck!"

"You are Scott?" Hunter queried.

"Yeah, but nobody calls me Scott," the boy responded. "I'm Rusty. It's swell you came so quickly."

"How old are you?" was Hunter's next question.

"I'll be twelve soon," Rusty answered. "How about you?"

"I'm going on fourteen," Hunter said.

"Well," said Rusty. "What do we do now?"

Hunter had had no time to plan, so he said, "I don't know. But you've got to have a bike."

"Dad gave me money to rent one for a week," Rusty told him, pulling out a worn wallet. "And here's the five dollars for you for today."

Hunter said that was too much for half a day, but Rusty made him take it.

They walked to Emmet's place, with Rusty looking around at everything. At the shop Rusty chose a red bike with ID number 314 painted in white on the back fender. When he paid for a week's rental, Emmet gave him a lock and key, telling him *never* to leave the bike unlocked.

"If you weren't with Hunter," he said, "I'd ask you for a deposit of thirty dollars."

Rusty's eyes widened in surprise. "How come?" he asked.

Emmet told him about the bicycles being stolen. Then he clapped one hand on Hunter's shoulder and announced, "And here's the guy who's going to catch the thief!"

"What d'you mean?" Rusty asked.

Hunter, feeling the blood rush to his face, told the other boy that he planned to stalk the thief and win the rewards, adding, "I need every buck I can earn."

"Hey!" Rusty burst out. "Can I help you — just for kicks?"

"I thought you wanted to see the sights," Hunter said.

Before Rusty could answer, Emmet spoke up. "Young fella, if you track the thief, and hunt for the missing bikes with Hunter, you'll see more of this island than any other tourist."

"All *right!*" Rusty shouted. "It's a deal. Let's get going."

The boys mounted and Rusty followed Hunter as he threaded his way among the horses, bicycles, pedestrians, and dogs that crowded Market Street.

"Whew!" Rusty called out. "It smells like a barn. Where are we going first?"

"The Pontiac Lookout," Hunter answered. "To plan strategy."

Rusty wrinkled his short nose. "What's a Pontiac doing on this island of no cars?" he queried.

Grinning, Hunter said. "He was a famous Indian chief. Grandfather told me his name was really Obwandiyag, but the whites called him Pontiac."

When they reached the cliff and had laid down their bikes, Rusty looked around and suddenly said, "Hey! Isn't this the place you were standing when I saw you through the binocs?"

Hunter nodded.

"Tell me," Rusty begged. "How did you disappear so fast? One second you were there and the next you had vanished!"

Hunter laughed, but didn't give away his secret.

Instead he pulled out his notebook and showed Rusty all the details he had learned from the four rental shops. Together they studied the facts and tried to figure out how the thief operated.

Privately owned bikes, it seemed, were in no danger. Only rentals had been stolen. And no rentals that were locked had been taken. That proved, the boys agreed, that the thief rode each bike from where he found it, but where he hid them was a mystery. No suspicious bikes had been seen on the ferryboats.

Only one bike disappeared in any one day. Why? Was the hideout so far away there wasn't time to snatch and hide a second one? The island wasn't really that big. Hunter suggested that maybe the thief came in his own small boat to the yacht club dock, and walked from there to one of the popular sights. Picking up a parked bike he might ride it to the dock, put it in his boat when no one was looking, and whiz away.

"That would account for one theft a day," Rusty said slowly. "But wouldn't people on the dock notice him and get wise to him?"

"Yeah, I guess so," Hunter agreed. "I think our best bet is that he sneaks the bike to his hideout, takes off the license tag and paints out the ID number so it can't be identified, and calls it a day."

"If he doesn't live on the island," Rusty said. "I wonder where he is staying?"

Both boys were quiet a while, and then Rusty asked, "Well, where do we begin, Sherlock?"

"We could begin to search the island for the hideout. I saw one possible place this morning," Hunter said. "Let's go and check it out."

Getting up and grabbing their bikes they set out along the West Bluff road. Before long they came to a large empty house with a porch on two sides. Because the land sloped, one end of the porch was only two feet above the lawn. The other end was six or seven feet high. In the lattice work that enclosed the area under the porch there was a door.

Hunter pointed out that bicycles could be stored under there, hidden by the thick ivy growing over the lattice. The thief could ride along the road, put the bike under the porch, and lock the door. He would have it made. The boys found there was a padlock on the door. Had the owner put it there — or the thief?

The boys began peering through the ivy leaves, pushing them apart with eager fingers. Under the porch it was dark. After rounding the corner, Hunter found a place where one root of the ivy had died. He pressed his face to the uncovered lattice and let out a yelp of excitement.

"What is it?" Rusty cried. "Let me see!"

"There's a big tarp covering something, and there's one bicycle wheel sticking out!"

Hunter stood aside to give Rusty a look.

"It's the missing bikes for sure!" the mainland boy yelled. "Man, you are tops! Shall we go and tell the police?"

"Not yet," Hunter cautioned. "We'd better check it out first. There's got to be a way to get in there, even if we have to dig."

They continued to circle the porch. At the farthest end they located a place where the lattice had been broken. The hole was only big enough for a small dog, but Rusty was quickly on his knees forcing his body through the opening. His shirt caught on a jagged piece of wood and he was stuck. He could not go ahead. He could not back out. Hunter had to break off a small slat. Then Rusty was free and moved forward. Hunter followed him. They crawled until there was room to stand up.

When they reached their goal they grinned at each other in the gloomy light. No doubt about it now. The heavy tarp covered several bicycles. Hunter could almost feel a thick wad of fifty one-dollar bills in his hand. Rusty reached out to lift the tarp.

"Hold it!" Hunter commanded. He had suddenly seen a way to win the whole hundred dollars. "We mustn't disturb anything. We don't want the thief to suspect anyone's been here. Then we'll figure out a way to trap him when he comes with another bike."

"Yeah," Rusty agreed unwillingly. "But shouldn't we just see if all the missing bikes are here?"

"I guess you're right," said Hunter. "But lift the cover easy."

In slow motion Rusty raised the tarp a foot or two. Then his face gradually turned red until it matched his hair. Only six bikes were there, and some of them were kids' bikes. All of them were coated with dust and laced together with spiderwebs. They must have been there for years.

"They're the wrong bikes!" Rusty cried.

Hunter felt like a pricked balloon. He didn't say a word as they made their way back to the outside. He was remembering other disappointments. Grandfather said you couldn't expect to win on the first try. By the time their bicycles were unlocked, Hunter was ready with a new plan.

He told Rusty about a big private estate called Stonecliffe, a couple of miles farther on. There was a mansion and a lodge for guests, also carriage houses, stables, barns, and workshops — lots of good places to hide stolen bikes.

"It sounds like a movie set," Rusty remarked. "But with so many people around, how could the thief escape being seen?"

Hunter answered, "The millionaires who built the

place died years ago. No one lives there now but a grouchy caretaker and his dog."

Rusty's eyes lighted up. "Great! But what if the caretaker sees us and sets his dog on us?"

"He won't!" Hunter promised. "I'll see to that."

A SUSPECT AND A SHOCK

As the boys cycled along the narrow woods road where the trees almost met overhead, Rusty asked Hunter what it was like to live on an island, and about his family. At first Hunter answered with a word or two. Then as he felt that the mainland boy was not just curious, but impressed and envious, he talked more freely. When he asked Rusty about his family the redhead said,

"There's nothing unusual or exciting about us. We're an ordinary family in an ordinary city. But Hunter, since you're a Native American, how come you don't have a name like — Tall Feather, or Sitting Bull? Martineau doesn't sound Indian."

Hunter answered, "One of my long ago grandfathers came from France. He was a fur-trader, and his name was Jacques Martineau. He married a woman in the Ottawa tribe, and all the rest of my family were Ottawas. My grandfather — that I lived with — was a chief."

Rusty's eyes widened. He would have asked more but at that point they came to the Stonecliffe entrance, marked by wrought-iron gates that blocked the road. They were not locked, but they carried a big printed notice:

PRIVATE PROPERTY
KEEP OUT
Trespassers will be prosecuted

"Oh-oh," Rusty said. "That looks bad."

"Forget it," Hunter answered. "I go through these woods any time I want."

When they had put their bikes out of sight Hunter glanced at his fellow-detective and frowned. "That yellow tee shirt of yours," he said, "is like a flag, to call people's attention."

Without hesitating, Rusty peeled off the shirt and flung it toward his bike. "How's this?" he asked.

Hunter laughed. He couldn't help it. "Not much better," he said. "I never saw such snow-white skin."

42

"Well, I can't take that off," Rusty growled.

"Try this," Hunter suggested, taking off his own dull green shirt and handing it to the redhead.

Rusty slipped it on and then stared with envy at Hunter's red-brown body. "Gee!" he remarked. "You're lucky. You've got natural camouflage!"

Next Hunter gave the other boy some tips on moving silently and invisibly through the trees. Rusty listened carefully, and as they moved off he tried to copy every move made by his guide.

They circled the mansion at a distance and saw no sign of the caretaker or his dog. Slipping from cover to cover they inspected the lodge and other buildings. After two hours they returned to the gates.

"Well," said Rusty as they got their bikes and he put on his own shirt, "we drew a blank, but it was neat fun learning those stalking tricks."

They were scarcely on their way when they heard the sound of horses' hoofs and the squeak of ungreased axles. Around the next curve the road was blocked by Kirby's team and big trash wagon. The boys moved to one side, but Kirby halted the horses.

"Hi, Hunter!" he called out. "Who's your friend?"

"This is Rusty," Hunter answered. "I — I'm showing him around."

"Hello there, Rusty," Kirby greeted him. "How do you like Mackinac?"

"It's cool!" Rusty answered, and full of enthusiasm added, "We're looking for the stolen bicycles!"

"Well!" Kirby exclaimed. "That's funny. Because — so am I!"

"*You are?*" Rusty was taken by surprise.

"Right!" And I have the best chance of finding them!" he boasted. "But you guys have fun anyway! So long!"

He clucked to his horses and moved on toward Stonecliffe.

Rusty, his face red, turned to the older boy. "Is that true?" he demanded.

Hunter nodded grimly. "I guess so. He drives every day to all the tourist spots, to empty the trash cans. Sooner or later he may pick up a clue, or see the thief taking a bike. Then all that dough will go in his pocket, not mine."

"Gee!" said Rusty. "What rotten luck."

Hunter went on. "I'm sorry you told him about us because now he'll try harder to beat us. Let's not tell anybody else."

"Not even my Dad?" Rusty asked.

"Oh sure. But nobody else. Okay?"

As they rode on in silence Rusty looked glum. To make him think of something else, Hunter told him about meeting Jancy and her aunt that morning, and taking them to Cragmore House.

It was close to supper time when Hunter and Rusty coasted downhill past the gleaming Grand Hotel, with its famous "longest porch in the world," and rode onto Lakeshore Boulevard. Hunter explained that this paved road circled the island at water level. They stopped so Rusty could see the wide pebbly area known as the Grand Hotel Beach. Dozens of people were sunning and splashing there.

"Say — can we swim here?" Rusty asked eagerly.

Hunter shrugged. "The water's shallow. Best place to swim is at the north end of the island, near British Landing. There's an old dock there, and deep water. Say!" he exclaimed. "Tomorrow let's bring our swim trunks along!"

"All *right*!" Rusty answered.

"We better bring sandwiches and pop too," Hunter added. "I guess someone at the Beacon Light can fix that for you."

As they were talking, a man on a rental passed them. Hunter hardly noticed him at first. Then something made him take a second look.

"Say, Rusty," he said excitedly. "Did you see anything funny about that guy?"

"Yeah," came the answer. "He's got a built-up shoe. Clubfoot, I guess. Or maybe polio."

"I didn't mean that," Hunter said. "He's riding a girl's bike!"

"So what?" said Rusty. "Maybe that's easier for a guy with a bad foot."

"Yeah, you could be right," Hunter answered.

They remounted and rode up Market Street. Just as they were passing Emmet's shop they saw a girl coming toward them on foot. She looked hot and out of breath. It was Jancy Southgate! They stopped. When Jancy reached them she cried out, "Hunter! Oh, Hunter! Am I glad to see you! The most awful thing has happened."

"What d'ya mean?"

The girl answered. "My bike was stolen. Will you go with me while I tell the man in the shop?"

"Sure," Hunter said to her, then to Rusty, "This is Jancy — I told you about her."

"Hi," he said. "I'm Rusty."

Locking their bikes, they went in and gave Emmet the news. He was upset and angry. "How did it happen?" he asked.

Holding back the tears Jancy said, "I was sketching Arch Rock, down on the shore, and when I turned around, the bicycle was gone."

"I told you to be careful," Emmet scolded her.

Rusty demanded, "Why didn't you give her a lock, like me?"

Scowling, Emmet told him he only had a few and there were no more to be bought on the island. To

Jancy he said, "I'm sorry, young lady. I'll have to keep your deposit money. But that won't buy me a new bike or make up for lost customers."

"I know," said Jancy admitted in a very small voice. "And I'm sorry for you. And for me too. All my spending money is gone."

An idea had been pricking at the back of Hunter's mind. "Jancy," he asked abruptly. "What color was your bike?"

"Black," she answered.

Hunter turned to the man. "Emmet, did you rent a girl's bike today — to a guy?"

Puzzled, the shopkeeper said, "No. I sure didn't. Why?"

Hunter asked another question. "What was Jancy's ID number?"

Emmet, opening his record book, said, "403. Why?"

"Well," Hunter answered. "A few minutes ago Rusty and I saw a fellow with a built-up shoe riding a *girl's* black bike, and I know the ID had a 4 in it. Could that be Jancy's bike?"

"Yipes!" Rusty yelped. "That's got to be it!"

"Come on!" Hunter said, grabbing his arm. "Let's go after him!"

Rusty glanced at his wristwatch and his face clouded. "I can't," he groaned. "I've got to meet Dad in a few minutes, and he's a nut about being on time."

"Then I'll go alone," Hunter said, starting for the door. "Can't waste any more time."

"When'll I see you?" Rusty wailed.

"Tomorrow about nine, at the Beacon Light. Remember sandwiches!"

"Gee," the redhead said gazing after Hunter. "I hope he gets him. But I wanted to be in on it!"

Jancy, her face full of new hope, asked Emmet, "Do you think Hunter will get him?"

The man shrugged. "'Tain't likely," he said.

Despair settled over the girl again. "If he doesn't, I'm sunk."

"Won't your aunt give you more money?" Rusty asked. "It wasn't your fault."

Shaking her head so her hair flew, she told him, "I don't think so. She wasn't keen on my riding around by myself."

"That's tough," Rusty agreed. "Maybe Hunter will think of something. I'll ask him in the morning."

"You're lucky to have Hunter to do things with," Jancy told him. "You're going to have a picnic tomorrow?"

"Yep. And swim at British Landing."

"Oh!" It was almost a wail. "I love to swim, almost as much as to paint and draw!"

Rusty looked at his watch again. "I've got to go,"

he said, "but we'll see what we can do for you."

Then he was out the door, on his bike, and away.

In the meantime Hunter was racing along Lakeshore Boulevard, avoiding people and pot holes by inches. When he reached the big shallow cave called Devil's Kitchen, he paused. Some tourists were having a picnic there. A quick glance showed that the handicapped rider was not among them.

Farther on there was a marker to show where the British had landed in 1812 and captured the island, in a surprise attack. Hunter stopped. Here the dirt road down the center of Mackinac met the paved boulevard. The guy might have gone on, or have turned into the smaller road. Hunter looked carefully, but there were no clear bike tracks. It was hopeless to go on. He would go home, get something to eat, and then ride to town for groceries.

At the old run-down house on the battlefield he turned into the little path, thinking how much had happened today. He whistled as he dropped his bike and unlocked the door. It sure was good to have his own place to come back to.

Inside, he gasped in horror and dismay. The back window had been smashed by a large rock that lay on the floor. Gleaming splinters of glass were on the floor and furniture. Fear knifed through the boy. Kirby had warned him that someone might break in and steal.

His eyes went to the nail where the owl headdress had always hung. He couldn't believe it. The headdress was still there! The ancient pottery bowl, the fragile peace pipe, and the arrowheads were still on the shelf where they belonged. Maybe he had arrived just in time to scare the would-be thief away!

He went outdoors and listened intently. There was no sound of a person running through the woods. At the back of the cabin, by the broken window, Hunter studied the ground. In the thick carpet of pine needles there were no traces. But in a small space where the earth was bare he found one clear print made by a heavy boot. One corner of the boot-heel was missing. If he saw that print again, anywhere, he could identify it!

If the guy didn't come to steal, why did he break the window? Would a stranger, or an island teenager, come this far off the beaten track and break a window for kicks?

Hunter didn't think so, but if things like this were going to happen, how could he keep the Indian treasures safe?

He knew he ought to clean up the broken glass, but he didn't feel like it. There were so many puzzles to sort out. Then suddenly Hunter remembered his grandfather saying, "Place your moccasins on the bit of the trail you can see. Take that step. The next one will be clear."

It was as if Grandfather had spoken. Hunter switched on the light and got the broom. After the floor had been swept clean, the boy's glance fell on the huge woodbox that stood between the stove and the window. Among the chunks of wood were bits of glass. That could be dangerous if he were to pick up a chunk carelessly. With a sigh he began lifting out the wood to get at the glass slivers. As he did this an idea hit him like the bursting of a Fourth of July rocket. This was the place for the treasures.

Slowly and carefully removing the glass bits, Hunter pulled out the sticks until they were all on the floor. Next he wrapped each article of Indian hand-craft in some of Grandfather's old clothing. When they were set in the bottom of the box, with more padding on top, Hunter put the wood back. The sticks that were left over, he took outside and added to the woodpile. Returning, he gazed at the box in triumph. It looked like a supply of wood for the stove and nothing else. He felt that Grandfather had led him to this hiding place.

Too tired now to return to town, Hunter opened a can of beans for his supper. As he climbed into bed a little later he remembered the man on the girl's bike.

Where should he and Rusty look for him tomorrow? And for the hidden bicycles? He couldn't decide, but he knew they had to find those bikes, or the thief, before Kirby did.

STAKE-OUT

B y seven o'clock the next morning Hunter was on his way to town. It was Saturday, and he had to do Mr. French's work early. He had mowed the lawn, and painted the lattice around the trash cans when Rusty saw him and came on the run. Today Rusty was wearing a brown shirt and jeans.

"Did you catch the guy?" he called.

Hunter was puzzled. How could Rusty know about the attack on the cabin? Then it dawned on him Rusty was asking about the man on a girl's bike. He told him what had happened.

"Wow!" the redhead exclaimed. "Now we have two mysteries! Did you write it in the notebook?"

Hunter said the broken window had nothing to do with the bike mystery. Rusty answered that you never knew. Maybe the thief was trying to scare Hunter into staying at home instead of hunting for the bicycles.

"He doesn't know I'm on his trail," Hunter objected.

Rusty made a face. "Maybe," he said, "but all the rental shop owners know, and word could have gotten around."

Hunter gave in. The boys sat on the hotel steps and added the new facts to the record.

"I think our next move," Hunter said, "is to find out if that clubfoot fellow rented that girl's bicycle at another shop. If he did, he's not a suspect, and if he didn't, we know who to look for!"

"Right!" Rusty agreed. "And it will be easy to spot him."

"Yeah," Hunter answered slowly. "That's one thing that makes me think he isn't the thief. It would be so stupid."

The boys' first stop was at Piperman's shop on Main street. No one there had seen the handicapped man. At Island House, the man Hunter had talked to the other day was not in the bike shed. In his place was a youth with a sour expression. When they asked if he had rented a girl's bike yesterday to a man with a built-up shoe, he grunted.

"I wouldn't know. This is my first day on the job and I hope it's my last. I wanted to drive horses."

"Where's the guy who was here?" Hunter questioned.

"He got sick and was took off to the hospital."

"Well, that's that," Rusty commented as they went back to the road.

Hunter pointed up to the East Bluff, directly above Island House, showing Rusty where Jancy lived.

"Say, Rusty," he asked. "What about Jancy? Will she rent another bike?"

"Nope. It's a crying shame. Here she is, without any friends but us, and no way to go anywhere except on foot. She's crazy about swimming, and if she had a bike she could go swimming with us. I know how my kid sister would feel."

"I never thought about that," Hunter remarked. "Maybe I could borrow a bike for her from Minnie."

"Who is Minnie?"

"My stepsister."

"Cool! Let's go and see about it. Pronto!"

"No," Hunter answered. "We've got to keep looking for those bicycles or Kirby will beat us to it."

"You've got something there," Rusty admitted. "We've still got the Grand Hotel Bike Shop to check out."

"We'll stop there later," Hunter said. "Now I want

to show you Arch Rock and then try a stake-out at Sugar Loaf."

As they pushed their bikes up the road to the top of the bluff Hunter told Rusty that, for Indians, Arch Rock and Sugar Loaf were the most important features of the island.

"How come?"

"Well," Hunter said, "the Indians didn't call it Arch Rock, but the Pierced Rock. The legend is that when the Great Spirit made his home on the Island of the Turtle, he pierced the rock there, to make an entrance."

Rusty wrinkled his colorful eyebrows. "The Island of the Turtle?" he queried.

"Mackinac means turtle in Indian. You see the island is oval, and it humps up in the middle."

Grinning, Rusty agreed it did look like a turtle.

The road twisted through woods thick with leafy trees and evergreens. The ground beside the road was brown with pine needles. It led to a large open space where lots of bicycles and carriages, big and small, were parked. The tourists were crowded against a low wall that guarded a steep rockslide.

Across the slide arched a natural bridge of weathered rock about fifty feet long. Everyone was looking at the Arch and through it at the jewel-like blue of the lake a hundred and fifty feet below. Others were on

56

the shore road, gazing up at the Arch. Rusty joined the crowd. Soon he spun around, his face shining.

"Hunter!" he cried. "This arch could not have been carved by a stream, so I think the legend is true. It's a Pierced Rock!"

Hunter grinned. He offered to hold Rusty's bike so he could go to the souvenir stand and buy a guidebook. When the redhead had that in his pocket Hunter pointed out that all the bushes under the trees here had been cleared out to make more parking space. There was no good spot here to hide and watch for the thief.

They set off on another road. Soon it joined a larger one that was noisy with the sound of wheels, horses' hoofs, and bursts of laughter from the passengers. There were cyclists too. At last this road made a loop around a solid cone of rock that towered seventy-five feet toward the sky. It was wide at the base and tapered to a point at the top.

"It looks like a teepee," Rusty commented.

"You're right," Hunter said. "Grandfather told me that the Great Spirit's teepee was originally made of deerskins. Later He turned it into rock, to remind us this was His sacred island. That's why the different tribes never fought here, but left their weapons on the mainland."

While Rusty explored the strange formation

Hunter looked for a hiding place. Soon they locked their bikes and slipped into the thick underbrush that bordered the road. Taking off their knapsacks they settled where they could see but not be seen.

"This is neat!" Rusty whispered.

Carriages were coming and going. Some passengers got out. Others craned their necks to look at Sugar Loaf while drivers droned facts and fancies about the rock. Bicycle riders dismounted and either laid their bikes at one side, or pushed them around the loop as they studied the unique rock.

Hunter was surprised to see a village kid named Greg ride into view. The ten-year-old towhead made the circuit of Sugar Loaf twice, apparently looking for someone or something. After he left, a man with lots of camera equipment arrived on a rented bike. He propped it against two litter cans at the edge of the road. Then he gave all his attention to taking pictures.

"This is just what I hoped for," Hunter said to his pal in a very low voice. "Here's a great chance for the thief!"

Before many minutes went by, a man came along, walking alone. He was a typical tourist with orange shorts, a loud shirt, and a crazy little hat. He was looking all around, not just at Sugar Loaf. Hunter held his breath. The man was in no hurry and stood aside as a buggy and some bicycles came by. When no others were in sight he moved on, then paused and seemed to stare at the photographer's bike. Hunter's heart beat fast and he grew tense. Rusty poked him. Then the visitor stooped down and gazed at a flower, a yellow lady-slipper, that grew under the bushes. After that he strolled on. Hunter let out his breath slowly. Rusty's disappointment showed on his face.

More carriages came, and cyclists, and pedestrians. Rusty began to wriggle. He looked at his watch, and held it up to his ear. To his surprise it was still running. Hunter, sitting cross-legged, was studying people just as he had learned to study wild creatures. To himself he said with a silent laugh, "Some of these tourists look pretty 'wild' to me!"

Rusty was wiggling again when Hunter heard squeaking axles. Around the curve came the trash dray. Hunter frowned. The trashman did have an advantage, and it didn't seem fair.

Kirby stopped his team by the overflowing cans, jumped down, and threw back the tarp that covered the dray's contents. He walked around, picking up bits of litter and tossing them into the dray. He studied the boys' bikes a minute, and looked around. Hunter decided to hide them, the next time they did a stakeout.

At last Kirby went toward the trash cans. Instead of wheeling away the rental that was parked there, he picked it up. Rusty gasped and jabbed Hunter with his finger. Kirby set the bike down against a tree, emptied the cans, replaced the tarp, and drove off.

"Wow!" Rusty said in Hunter's ear. "I thought he was going to put it in the wagon!"

"Nuts!" Hunter whispered back. "He's looking for the thief, same as we are."

"Can we go swimming now?" Rusty asked. "My legs are full of pins."

"I s'pose so," Hunter said. So they picked up their knapsacks and came out of hiding.

Hunter led the way to the road down the center of the island, and turned toward British Landing. When they reached the Battlefield he pointed out the trail to his cabin. Rusty skidded to a stop.

"Hey! Can we go there?" he begged. "It would be cool to see the Indian things you told me about!"

"Not today," Hunter answered, "but come on. Here's something you mustn't miss," showing him the marker. It detailed the history of the 1814 battle when the Americans tried to recapture the island and were defeated by the British and their Indian allies. After Rusty had read that gory tale he looked at the old house that had sheltered the wounded.

"Wow!" he exclaimed. "That looks ready to collapse!"

A shout from up the road startled both boys.

"Hunter! Hunter! Wait for me!"

It was that village kid, Greg, coming down the hill fast.

"What's the matter?" Hunter asked as the boy stopped beside them.

"Nothin'. I wanted to come with you."

"Look, Greg, I'm showing Rusty the island. You'd be bored stiff."

"No, I wouldn't," Greg insisted. "Mr. Clemson says you know more about the island than any kid in school. Let me go with you!"

Hunter felt something was goofy, but before he spoke, Rusty said, "He might as well come swimming with us."

"Okay," Hunter agreed, but he had an uneasy feeling about the kid.

QUESTIONS WITHOUT ANSWERS

When the three boys reached the remains of the old dock, Rusty's eyes widened in amazement. "It's humongous!" he exclaimed. "Was it built for the British warships to land at?"

Greg doubled up laughing.

"No," Hunter answered, keeping his face straight. "The British came from their ship in little boats. This dock was built much later, for the big lake steamers. It hasn't been used for ages."

Though the great pilings looked strong, most of the framework and planking had rotted. The boys picked their way around gaping holes out to the end where the crystal clear water was at least twenty feet deep. In another minute they were diving in, climbing out, and going in again with huge splashes.

After a while they were hungry. They sat on the end of the dock, sharing their sandwiches with Greg. As they ate, Rusty was reading his guidebook and Greg was peppering Hunter with questions. Where had he and the redhead been so far? What had they seen? Where were they going next? Hunter gave short answers or just said, "I dunno."

When Greg asked if they had seen anything unusual, it was Rusty who answered.

"Yeah. That wreck of a house on the battlefield. It's not cared for like the old buildings downtown, or the Fort. Why don't they fix it up?"

"Oh," Hunter told him. "It's too far gone to repair. They don't tear it down because it's a landmark."

"And it's haunted!" Greg chimed in.

"You're crazy," laughed Rusty.

"No! Honest. It *is* haunted." Greg insisted. "It's haunted by ghosts of soldiers killed in that battle. A couple of guys in the village tried to sleep there once, to win a bet. They scrammed when they saw a soldier coming down the stairs with his scalp gone!"

"Man-oh-man!" said Rusty. "That place I've got to explore!"

As soon as they had finished eating, the boys chased each other into the water again. Under the dock they found a huge floating log which they tugged out into the open. They rode it, they paddled it, and tried to stand on it the way loggers do.

Every once in a while Hunter whispered to Rusty that they ought to get on with the bicycle hunt. Rusty begged to stay a little longer.

It was late afternoon when they finally dressed. Rusty wanted to go back on the center road so he could go in the ghost house. Greg said it was too hot to ride up that hill, and said it would be easier to go back along the west shore.

"No," Hunter decided. "We'll go the other way, so Rusty can see the east shore and look up at Arch Rock from the lake."

"It's funny!" Rusty said, laughing. "We can go east or west to get home!"

They followed the road northwest to Pine Point. After making the sharp turn there, Rusty called attention to a narrow graveled track that disappeared into the woods.

"That looks mysterious," he announced. "Maybe we ought to look into it."

"Why?" Greg asked.

Hunter said to the redhead, "You've got a runaway imagination. That goes to a private home."

"Islanders or summer people?" Rusty asked.

"Neither, really. It's a retired professor named

Witsorek, and his daughter. They come as soon as the ice is gone and stay until the lake freezes again. I've seen Miss Witsorek a couple of times, at the grocery store, but never her father. He's always writing books."

"Oh, a hermit!" Rusty exclaimed.

"What's a hermit?" Greg asked eagerly.

"A guy who doesn't want people snooping around," Rusty said, and Greg looked disappointed.

At Arch Rock they stopped only for a minute and then went on to town. Hunter reminded Rusty they had to go to the Grand Hotel.

"What for?" Greg asked.

With a solemn face Rusty answered, "We're thinking of buying the joint."

That shut Greg up for a few minutes.

The bike shop was at the back of the imposing hotel. Stopping there, Hunter said,

"Rusty, you and Greg can stay out here with the bikes. Okay?"

"Sure. You go in and ask the question."

As Hunter walked away he heard Greg ask Rusty, "What question?"

"Greg," the redhead declared, "you're as full of questions as a T.V. quiz show."

In a short time Hunter came out and winked at his partner.

"They never saw him," he reported. "So now we know!"

"Never saw who?" Greg demanded.

Hunter told the boy to go home. He and Rusty were going back to the Beacon Light. Greg made no move to follow them, but stayed where he was until they were out of sight.

As soon as it was safe, Rusty asked, "You really think the clubfoot guy is the thief?"

"Sure looks like it. We saw him riding a rented bike, but no rental shop men have seen him. They couldn't miss a guy with a shoe like that."

Hunter was thoughtful. Then he said, "You know, Rusty, I get an uncomfortable feeling about that kid, Greg."

"Me too." Rusty agreed. "Bad vibes."

"If he tags along tomorrow we'll give him the slip."

At the Beacon Light they saw a big athletic looking man coming out onto the porch.

"Dad! Oh Dad!" Rusty called. "Have I got a lot to tell you! And here is Hunter!"

Rusty's Dad had strong features with blue eyes like his son's, and sandy-gray hair. He came down and shook Hunter's hand.

"I'm glad to meet you, Hunter," he said. "You're sure giving Rusty a whale of a time."

Hunter, not knowing what to say, returned the handshake and smiled.

"I was hoping to see you," the man went on. "Tomorrow is Sunday and all our bunch is taking a charter boat trip to the Snow Islands. You can have the day off, or you could come along as our guest."

Rusty begged him to do that, but Hunter said he had lots of things to do.

"Well, then," Mr. Hammergren said. "We want you to have dinner with us here on Tuesday. We'll invite Jancy and her aunt, and all go to the movies."

That invitation Hunter accepted. Suddenly he realized what a lot the Hammergrens were doing for him. He knew his grandfather would want him to show hospitality too. He spoke up quickly before he could change his mind.

"After the movies," he said. "Could Rusty come and spend the night with me in Grandfather's cabin?"

Rusty let out a whoop, and his Dad, after asking a few questions, said he could go. Hunter picked up his bicycle.

"While you're at the Snows," he promised, "I'll be working on the mystery. See ya!"

He bought his groceries and a pane of glass, and went home. Approaching the cabin he felt a tingle of fear. Had there been more vandalism while he was away all day?

To his relief everything was all right. As he repaired the window and got his supper he made plans for the next day. Sunday was the busiest tourist day and he was going to make the most of it. He decided to do a stake-out at Arch Rock, down by the lake.

Then he stepped outside into the soft twilight. A few birds were calling but they sounded sleepy. The air smelled of pines and cedars. He strolled down the path listening to the whisperings of the forest. This stillness, alive with the sounds of birds and animals and insects, he would never experience if he lived in the village.

By the time he reached the road it was deep dusk. Before turning back he glanced across at the empty house. Against the night sky it was only a shabby, cardboard outline. Then a low shadow detached itself from the side of the house and scurried through the meadow grass toward the trees beyond. Hunter stiffened and stared. What in the world? It was too solid for a ghost and it didn't leap like a deer. Too broad for a dog. What could it be?

At the edge of the woods the shadow suddenly chaged shape. It seemed to unfold. It was a man! He had been running bent over. What was he doing and why was he acting afraid?

With a quick shiver Hunter wondered if he had set the historic house on fire. There were people, he knew, who did that kind of thing. That old building would go up in flames like paper.

Scenting the air like a hound, Hunter thought maybe he did smell smoke. He ran lightly across the road and onto the rickety porch. There was no flickering red glow anywhere inside, and no smoke either. He looked again toward the woods.

The man had disappeared, but Hunter noted the exact spot where he had been. Next day he would examine the ground there.

Walking back to the cabin Hunter wondered if this was the vandal who had smashed his window. If he found the mark of a broken heel he would know for sure.

In the morning Hunter returned to the haunted house. He easily followed the bent grasses and weeds where the fleeing man had stepped. The ground there and under the trees was too dry to show footprints, but Hunter felt sure the guy had worn soft shoes, not heavy boots. He grinned, thinking how interested Rusty would be in still another mystery.

Now he could spend the rest of the day looking for the thief. At Arch Rock Hunter settled into his lookout post before the first sightseers arrived. Soon hordes of them began to come, and kept on coming. It was a hot day. Many bicycles were left alone while their riders gazed in awe and took pictures. Two or three hours went by. The thief had not shown up.

"Just my luck," Hunter thought. "To have the guy snatch one from the hotel beach or Sugar Loaf today."

Greg appeared. He stopped and looked around, and then rode on toward Pine Point. What *was* the kid doing?

Hunter took out his notebook and studied it. Since the information had come from four shops it was hard to get an over-all picture. On a new page he listed, in order, the date, time, and place each bike had disappeared.

Two days in a row the Grand Hotel Beach had been victimized. Then not again for a week. Bikes had disappeared from Arch Rock every two or three days. In between, the thief had been busy at Sugar Loaf or the Fort. One bike had vanished from a lonely woods road while its rider wandered off looking for wildflowers.

He studied the dates again and came up with a fact that astounded him. No bikes had been stolen on Sundays. Was it only chance, or was there a reason? Did it mean the thief had a job on Sunday? Hunter remembered hearing that extra men were hired to drive tourist rigs on Sundays. Was one of them the thief, doing his sneaky business on weekdays, and driving like an honest man each Sunday?

Busy with these puzzles, Hunter had not kept watch of the road. It was only by luck that he looked up just in time to see a man on a green tenspeed whiz by, headed for town. It was a rental, and the rider wore a built-up shoe.

Hunter, scrambling to his feet, rushed across the road where he had left his bike behind a boulder. He reached in his pocket for the key but it was not there. In a flash he realized it could have slipped out along with the notebook. Back to his hiding place he ran. At first he saw nothing, and began to panic. Then as he looked closely, a gleam of metal caught his eye. The key had fallen between two big rocks. It was hard to get out, but finally he had it and went racing after the suspect.

Rounding the corner under the cliff called Robinson's Folly, he looked at the straight road ahead. There was no sign of the rider. He rode on. The zigzag street up to the East Bluff was empty too. At Marquette Park Hunter stopped. Where to look now? Main Street or Market? He remembered seeing the man passing the Beach the other day, so his hideout must be in that direction. Hunter sped along Market Street to the lakeshore.

At the Beach the only bike in sight was coming toward him. It was Greg. Hunter stopped and called out, "Say, did you meet a guy on a green tenspeed? Riding fast?"

"Unh-unh," Greg answered. "Why?"

"Never mind," Hunter snapped, "and quit bug-

71

ging me."

It was no use looking farther. He headed for the village to see his Dad, who sometimes had Sunday off from his work in the stables.

Bella and the children were on the porch of their box-like house, trying to keep cool.

"Hi," Hunter said. "Where's Dad?"

"In the backyard," his stepmother answered, so Hunter walked around the house.

In a minute he and Tim came back together. Hunter was two inches taller than his Dad, straight and slender. Timber had a chest like a barrel, and was strong, but due to an accident years before, he was bent and walked with an awkward jerk.

Looking at them and shaking her head, Bella laughed. "No one would ever guess you are father and son. Even your skin color is different!"

Minnie spoke up from the corner where she and Adele were squabbling over Barbie dolls. "They both got black hair!" she said.

"But even that is different," Bella insisted. "Tim's hair is soft and curly, but Hunter's is smooth and stiff."

"Oh well," said Tim, "the librarian says I am a throwback to the French fur-trapper, but Hunter is all Indian, like the Old Chief."

Bella, her yellow hair damp around her pale face,

slumped back in her rocking chair. "Well, Indian or French, it don't make us no cooler."

On the floor at her feet six-month old Sam was playing with her loose shoe laces. He was wearing only diapers, and Hunter grinned to see the warm brown color of his skin. It looked just right with his cap of straight black hair. Sam was Indian, even if his mother wasn't.

Hunter picked up the baby and sat down on the step next to his Dad. Sam opened his bud of a mouth, squeezing his fat cheeks up so tight that his eyes were hidden. Hunter steeled himself for a mighty yell, but none came. Instead, the round black eyes opened again and gazed intently at Hunter. The mouth closed. Then the red lips parted in a smile. Hunter's heart did a flip-flop. The baby knew him, liked him!

Timber asked Hunter how he was getting on for jobs, so Hunter told him about showing Rusty the island. He told about helping Mrs. DuPont, and Jancy's hard luck with her rental. He asked Minnie, who was ten, if Jancy could use her bike for a week or so. The little girl hesitated, but when Hunter offered her a couple of candy bars she said okay.

Then Kirby came by and stopped to chat. As he leaned against the porch and pulled out a pack of cigarettes, a small piece of paper fluttered to the ground. He paid no attention but Hunter, who couldn't stand litter, picked up the scrap and crumpled it into his pocket.

Bella asked Hunter to stay for lunch but he wanted to get going. Soon he rode off, grasping the second bike by the center of the handlebars.

At Cragmore House Hunter knocked on the screen door.

"Oh!" Jancy exclaimed as she opened it. "Do you have my stolen bike?"

"N-no," Hunter said slowly.

"Well, come in anyway. I think Aunt Myra wants to see you."

Hunter couldn't think why, but followed Jancy to the dining room. Mrs. DuPont smiled and told him to sit down.

"Jancy," she said, passing him a plate of cookies. "Bring this young man a glass of milk."

"Thanks," Hunter said, puzzled.

Mrs. DuPont started to explain. "I had the telephone connected," she said. "and the first call I had was from a man named Hammergren. Do you know him?"

"Yes Ma'am."

"He told me you are showing his son around the island."

Hunter nodded.

"Mr. Hammergren felt sorry for Jancy because her bike was stolen. He invited her — and me — for dinner and the movies Tuesday night. I don't feel up to going. Before I let Jancy accept the invitation, I'm glad to talk with you. What kind of man is Mr. Hammergren?"

Hunter hesitated. Then he said. "I liked him right away. I — I think he's a man my grandfather would have liked — and trusted."

"What about his boy Scott?"

Jancy grinned. "Aunt Myra, you *can't* call him Scott. He's just Rusty!"

Mrs. DuPont raised her eyebrows and looked questioningly at Hunter.

Again the boy paused before answering. "I like Rusty," he said. "He's friendly. He doesn't think he knows everything. He's fun, and he likes to see and learn new things."

"He's not wild like some youngsters these days?" Mrs. DuPont asked.

"Oh, no," came the quick answer.

"Aunt Myra," Jancy put in eagerly, "I've just remembered! Rusty was dying to go with Hunter to chase the man who stole my bike. He didn't go, because he had promised his Dad to be back at a certain time!"

Mrs. DuPont smiled. "That's a good point," she admitted. "Well, Mr. Hammergren says he will escort Jancy home Tuesday, so I think maybe it will be all right."

Her niece's brown eyes sparkled. "That will make up a bit for other things I'm missing," she said.

That reminded Hunter why he had come.

"I borrowed my stepsister's bike for you to use," he said. "It's outside."

The girl's face grew rosy with pleasure. "How super!" she said. "Thank you! Can I get a lock for it?"

"Maybe," Hunter told her. "But it's old and rusted, and only rentals have been stolen."

"Oh, Aunt Myra," she exclaimed. "Now I can go places!"

Mrs. DuPont gave a worried sigh. "I wish you didn't have to go alone," she said.

Hunter screwed up his courage to ask, "Mrs. DuPont, if Rusty and I come here tomorrow afternoon, could Jancy ride with us to British Landing for a swim? We'll show her a lot of the island!"

"Please say yes!!" Jancy begged her aunt. "Remember, I've been swimming since I was little, and I've passed Red Cross Junior Life Saving! Please, Aunt Myra?"

Finally Mrs. DuPont agreed. Soon Hunter rode off, feeling things had turned out well.

He headed for home, eager to do some bird-watching. If no bikes were stolen on Sundays, why waste the afternoon waiting for the thief to show up?

THE SPY

At home, after a quick lunch, Hunter slipped the strap of the glasses around his neck and set out. High in the branches he heard the "tsee-tsee-tseet!" of a redstart. Soon he saw the tiny black and red warbler as it darted nervously from tree to tree. He was so intent that he hardly noticed when the bird led him across the road, and then back near the haunted house. Suddenly a voice said,

"Hi, Hunter!"

Hunter lowered the glasses and saw Kirby Tyson standing by the porch. The dray was nowhere to be seen.

"How did you get here?" the boy asked.

"On my bike," came the answer. "This is my Sunday off and I've been checking some clues on those stolen bicycles. Just stopped for a smoke." Then pointing to the glasses he asked, "Where'd you get those fancy binoculars?"

Hunter tried to speak but couldn't.

"Never mind," Kirby went on. "The more time you hunt birds, the better *my* chances are. And I have an idea about the binocs."

"They belong to a friend," Hunter managed to say, but his mind was in a whirl as he crossed the road and followed the trail home. He slumped on Grandfather's bed. How could Kirby guess his secret? Nobody knew. Hunter began to go over in his mind what had happened a few weeks ago.

The binoculars were always on Mr. Clemson's desk. One Friday Hunter had accidently knocked them into the scrap basket. Nobody was in the room. Instead of taking them out, Hunter had covered them with paper. Later he had emptied the basket into the dumpster behind the school, and had slipped the glasses into his knapsack. He had told himself he would borrow them, and give them back later. By Monday Mr. Clemson missed the glasses. After fruitless search and questioning, the teacher remarked that they might have gone out with the trash. He would ask Tyson to look for them at the landfill. So that must be how Kirby knew the glasses were missing. Today the trashman had put two and two together. Would he tell anybody?

Hunter realized the glasses were worth a lot of money, and wished with all his heart he had never "borrowed" them. Well, he wouldn't use them anymore. He went out and hid them again in the hole in the cedar tree. He would return them just as soon as he could figure a way to do it without getting caught and sent to jail.

In the morning Hunter was still worried. Solving the bicycle mystery didn't seem so exciting. Still, he needed the money. Remembering the handicapped man on the ten-speed he decided to stop at the police booth before meeting Rusty.

The officer on duty there said no stolen bicycles had been reported the day before.

"But I saw a man on a bike I think was stolen!" Hunter told him. "It was a green ten-speed."

The policeman re-checked his clipboard and shook his head.

"A ten-speed was stolen Saturday, but none yesterday."

To himself Hunter said, "Never on Sunday. That's three weeks in a row. I wonder where that handicapped guy got the green bike he was riding?"

He asked more questions and wrote down the

latest details. As he went on to the Beacon Light he was puzzling over the riddle of Sundays. If he could solve that, it would help identify the thief.

Rusty burst out of the hotel. "What's new?" he asked.

"Plenty," Hunter said. "Let's go down by the water and I'll tell you."

Rusty groaned over the second disappearance of the man with the built-up shoe. Why was he on a different bike this time? Like Hunter he was mystified by "no thefts on Sundays". He cheered when he heard that Jancy now had a bike to use and could go swimming with them.

Hunter asked Rusty how his trip was.

"Not bad," the other boy said. "It got kind of boring, but on the way back we had a ball!"

He reported that a well-known entertainer had performed for the crowd on the charter boat, doing take-offs of famous people.

"He did Bob Hope, and the president, and Carol Burnett, and lots more!" Rusty cried. "We were rolling off our chairs. He sounded and acted exactly like each one. Wish you could hear him."

"If it was Jim Redding, I have," Hunter said.

"How come?"

"He's an islander," Hunter answered. "He's away most of the time, but when he's at home he puts on a show for us. The roof flies off when he mimics the Fudgies!"

When Rusty asked, "What do we do next?" Hunter was ready with a plan.

"You've got to see the Fort," he announced, "and this is a good day for that. While you're inside looking at the exhibits I'll be keeping a watch on rented bikes outside."

Leaving their wheels behind the library they walked up the steep street toward the Fort. They were joined by Greg pushing his bike. Annoyed, Hunter said,

"What is it with you, Greg, always tailing along?"

Turning red the towhead answered, "I just like to be with you."

When he heard tht Rusty was going into the Fort, he said he would stick with Hunter.

"No way!" Hunter replied. "Get lost."

"I can follow you," the boy said stubbornly.

"Just try it!" Hunter challenged him.

He took Rusty aside to whisper that he would meet him on the parade ground in about two hours. Rusty joined the tourists crowding up a ramp that led to the south gate of the Fort. Many had left bicycles in a rack at the foot of the ramp. Across the street stood a stone church with double doors.

That was where Hunter planned to keep watch,

but he walked down Market Street with Greg tailing him. Suddenly Hunter sprinted around the back of the church, dodging through trees and shrubs. He saw Greg drop his bike to run after him. Quickly Hunter circled the small building, popped inside the doors and stopped them from swinging. Peeking through the crack he could see the towhead on the sidewalk, looking up and down the street, his mouth open in amazement.

Hunter grinned and waited until Greg went away. Through the glass in the upper part of the doors he could watch tourists leaving their bikes in the rack. He observed them carefully, so he would know if a different person took a bike.

There was so much to see that the two hours passed quickly. It was time to meet Rusty. Hunter went up to the parade ground on the far side of the Fort and stood by the gate, waiting. Suddenly, past the blockhouse at the far end of the Fort wall he saw Greg's yellow head, peering around. Like a shot Hunter was after him but by the time he got there Greg was on his bike speeding down toward Main Street. Why was the kid shadowing him? What was he after?

When Rusty came out he said, "That's one of the best things I've ever seen! It's like being in a time clock, and stepping out at different times when exciting things were happening at the Fort. Those life-size figures in costume and the old-time settings were cool!"

Hunter suggested they go down to one of the ferry docks and eat their sandwiches there. So they did, dangling their feet over the water and watching great oreboats loaded with grain or iron-ore threading their way between Mackinac and Round Island, while smaller craft kept out of their path. A breeze swept over the boys and waved the flags on the ferries going to and from the mainland, each making its solemn and ear-splitting toot as it approached or took off.

When the boys had finished eating, Hunter took out the notebook to bring his partner up to date. Out flew a small piece of paper. Hunter grabbed it. He was about to stuff it in with the lunch trash when suddenly he smoothed it out and bent over it. Rusty looked too. There was a message written in a childish scrawl:

They didn't hunt for no bikes. All they done was swim. At the Grand Hotel Bike Shop they asked about a crippul riding a bike. Maybe he is the theef.

Greg.

Hunter froze with fury. Greg was tailing them and reporting to Kirby!

Rusty asked, "Where did you get this?"

"Kirby dropped it at Dad's house. I picked it up to throw away."

"How come Greg knew what you said to the man in the shop?" Rusty wondered aloud.

Hunter answered, "The fink went in and talked to the guy after we left, I guess."

Rusty leaped to his feet, his freckled face flaming.

"A spy! I'd like to mash that lousy kid!" he yelled, jumping up and down in anger.

One foot slipped off the edge of the dock. Rusty waved his arms but could not regain his balance. He went cartwheeling through the air. There was a big splash as he hit the water eight feet below.

Hunter couldn't help laughing when the curly red head came to the surface. "That's one way to cool it!" he called out.

Rusty said nothing. Weighed down by his jeans and shoes he began the slow swim to shore. Hunter picked up both knapsacks and went to meet him. Together they hurried to the Beacon Light, discussing what to do with Greg. Rusty got into dry things and then checked his watch.

"Hey! It's still running!" he cried. "And it's time to go and get Jancy."

Walking to the library for their bikes, Hunter remembered to tell Rusty about the figure he had seen last night running away from the haunted house.

"Gee!" Rusty responded enviously. "Kooky things happen at your place. I hope they do tomorrow night when I'm there with you!"

A CLUE AND A
CLOSED DOOR

As Hunter and Rusty unlocked their bikes they saw Greg a block away watching them. Rusty wanted to go and beat him up.

"No," Hunter said. "We'll just give him the slip and then go to Jan's house."

They walked their bikes up the steep street between the Fort and the church. Greg was following.

"Across from the parade ground," Hunter told Rusty, "is the governor's mansion. There's a big shed. We'll slip inside and hide until Greg has gone by. He'll think we're on our way to the West Bluff."

"How will we get to the East Bluff?"

"Easy. There's a shortcut I'll show you."

At just the right place, a curve in the street hid them from Greg's view so they got into the shed unseen by him. From their shelter the boys watched Greg come up the hill. He mounted his bike and rode by looking pleased with himself.

Rusty snickered quietly. "Wonder how far he'll go before he finds he's not following us!"

"Several miles, I hope!" Hunter answered.

As they rode to the East Bluff the boys decided it would be fun to tell Jancy they were trying to catch the thief and find the bicycles. She might get a kick out of it.

When they reached her house Jancy came running out, full of eagerness, wearing blue shorts and a blue and white top. Her shining hair sported a small blue scarf. Picking up Minnie's bike, she put her towel in the basket.

"Got your suit?" Rusty asked.

"Under my shorts," she answered. "This is going to be fun!"

"Wait till you hear the real fun!" Rusty said. "Hunter and I are on the trail of the mysterious bicycle thief. Don't tell anybody but — "

"Oh super!" Jancy squealed with excitement. "I read all the Nancy Drew mysteries! Have you any clues? Can I help?"

The three set off together, Hunter leading the way

and Rusty telling Jancy about the second disappearance of the handicapped rider — on a different bike! And about Greg spying for Kirby.

At Sugar Loaf they stopped, and Hunter stayed with the bikes while Rusty showed Jan the Rock Teepee and told her its story. Just as the other two joined him, Hunter saw Greg in the distance. He scowled. Somehow the kid had discovered he was on a false trail and was looking for them once more.

"Don't look now," Hunter told his friends. "But our shadow has caught up with us. We'll have to lose him again. I'll ride ahead. When I hold up my hand, do exactly what I do. Fast!"

The road they followed wound like a snake's track through the woods. After rounding an extra-sharp curve Hunter held up one hand, leaped off his bike and dragged it into the thick tangle of bushes at one side. Rusty and Jan did the same, bubbling with suppressed laughter. They all lay quiet, hidden.

Hunter wriggled forward on his stomach until he could see the road as it approached the corner. He kept his head low, eyes on the road. Soon Greg came along, slowed up, and got off his bike. Hunter almost stopped breathing. Greg wasn't an Indian and couldn't read tracks. What was he doing? Carefully Greg peeked around the corner, and then rode on again. Oh! He didn't want to be seen; that was it!

As soon as Greg had disappeared Rusty sat up, ready to go. Hunter said they must give Greg ten minutes to get to the Harrisonville crossroads and decide where to go next. Hunter used the time to record in his notebook about Greg's spying for Kirby, and how they had thrown him off their track. Rusty told Jan more about their detective work and about the haunted house.

At last Hunter said they could move on. When they came to the crossroads, Hunter studied the tracks made by Greg's tires. Luckily there had been no traffic since he was there.

"He started toward British Landing," Hunter reported. "Then he went a few yards toward the village, changed his mind, and finally rode back to town."

"Hooray!" Rusty sang out.

"Hunter," Jan said admiringly, "you read tracks the way the rest of us read road signs!"

They took the road to the Landing. At the battlefield marker they stopped for a look at the haunted house. It was a sorry wreck. The roof had caved in where a tree had fallen on it, and the walls were sagging. One support of the porch had rotted away, giving it a drunken look.

While others were taking all this in, Hunter noticed a narrow path worn through the tall dried grass. It went around to the back of the house. It was not an animal trail. Curious, Hunter followed it, with the others at his heels. It led to a basement door which had no handle. Hunter pushed against it but nothing happened. All three kids leaned against it as hard as they could. The door did not budge.

"That's weird," Hunter said. "Last summer this door was open, hanging on one hinge. I suppose the Mackinac Commission had it shut for safety. But somebody's been going in and out. This path is being used."

"Let's go in, and down the stairs!" Jan suggested.

Hunter answered, "There aren't any stairs to the basement."

"There have to be stairs," Jancy insisted.

"You're right!" Rusty agreed. "Let's go in and find them."

Hunter shrugged.

The kids returned to the porch. The front door was locked but there were big windows from which the glass was long gone.

"Is it safe to go in?" Jancy asked.

"Sure," Hunter said. "Ghosts don't bug you in the daytime."

Rusty climbed in first and helped Jan. Just as her feet touched the floor a high-pitched, eerie screech rang through the house. The two kids turned stiff as stone. Terrified, Jancy clutched Rusty's hand. His freckles stood out on his fair skin like pepper on a fried egg. Hunter, grinning, did not move for a long minute. Then he came through the window and laid a hand on Rusty's shoulder.

"It's only bats — up under the roof!" he said.

"Bats!" Jancy screamed. "That's worse than ghosts!"

After that the kids surveyed the room. On the ragged remains of a large rug stood a lop-sided rocking chair with only one rocker. Also a chair with a broken leg and no seat. Jagged pieces of glass, cigarette butts, beer cans, and dirt littered the floor. Jancy wrinkled her nose in disgust.

"I didn't know ghosts were so messy!" she said.

Watching where they put their feet, the three went exploring. They opened every door and poked in every closet but found no stairs to the basement. Rusty was stumped.

"You were right, Hunter," he admitted. "There's no way to go down. But let's go up to the second floor and look around."

Hunter vetoed that. The stairs were too dangerous, he said. The wooden supports were rotten and some of the treads were missing.

"Besides," Jancy added with a grin. "We'd stir up those ghosts again!"

At that moment there was another spine-tingling shriek from the roof.

"Let's get out of here," she said.

As they picked up their bikes she turned back for another look. "That's a real haunted house," she announced. "I'd like to sketch it. I'll draw the living room with a ghost floating down the missing stairs, and another one sitting on that bottomless chair!"

"Put in the bats," Rusty suggested, "for sound effects!"

Those two seemed to have forgotten the mystery of that path to the closed door, but Hunter was puzzling over it until they got to the lake.

The afternoon sun was shining on the lake, making it the bluest of blues. Before long all three were in the water. The boys were awed to see what a good swimmer and beautiful diver Jancy was. They were having a ball.

In a few minutes a lively family of tourists arrived. They left their rented bikes by the road and joined in the fun. Everybody was having such fun together that even Hunter forgot the new mystery at the haunted house.

Finally the father told his family to sit in the sun and dry off. Jancy asked the time, and said she ought to get dry too. The family and the three friends sat together on the dock and began asking Hunter about Mackinac. They listened, fascinated, to his stories of Indians, French, British, and Americans who had shared the history of the island.

At last they had to break it up. The younger boy went to the road where he had left his green rental leaning against a tree.

"Where's my bike?" he asked.

Hunter and Rusty sprang to their feet. Frantic searching by the whole group turned up no trace of the missing bicycle. Rusty turned as red as a cardinal bird.

"That thief has taken a bike right under our noses!" he yelled. "It makes me mad."

Jancy said to the small boy, "I know *exactly* how you feel. My bike was stolen too."

It was a saddened family that went off to report their loss, with the boy riding on his Dad's crossbar.

"Well," Hunter said. "We've another chance to track the thief to his hideout, but which way did he go? I bet on the center road."

"Oh, no!" Rusty protested. "That's steep and slow. I'm sure he'd go the way we did the other day, around Pine Point. You can really speed there."

"Let's make a two-pronged attack," Hunter suggested. "You go that way and I'll go the other. Jancy, which way would you like to go?"

"I better take the fast way," she said. "Aunt Myra will be expecting me."

As soon as the other two had started, Hunter took one more look where the boy's bike had been parked. On the brown grass beside the road were a few tiny spots of bright green. Hunter touched them, and his finger tip was green.

"Paint!" he said to himself. "I bet he used spray paint on the ID number. Now it's like he's riding a private bike with only the license tag. If Rusty and Jan see him they won't know that's the stolen bike."

Then he shouted. "Wahoo! I've found out one thing about the way the thief works!"

Hunter set off at top speed for the center road where he met several tourist rigs and cyclists. He also met Kirby coming away from the dump. There was no sign of the thief. Once more he had done the disappearing act. Hot and discouraged, Hunter headed home.

When he reached the path to the cabin he saw a large tourist carry-all stopped in front of the haunted house. The passengers were reading the historic marker, and the driver added a few dramatic touches to the story. Hunter, listening, grinned to himself. Then a movement at the back of the house caught his eye. A low, crouching figure took a quick look at the departing tourists and then drew back out of sight. Hunter was electrified. It looked like the same guy he had seen there last night. What *was* he doing?

Dropping his bike, Hunter ran to the back of the house. He was just in time to see the fellow get on a bicycle and whiz around the far corner. Hunter rushed after him. In his excitement and hurry he stumbled on the rough ground and took a headlong spill. He wasn't hurt but he had lost precious seconds.

When he got to where he could see, the man was riding furiously down toward the shore road. He was perhaps fifty yards away but Hunter could see that the bike was green and had no ID number on the back fender. The man was bent double and had a visor cap pulled low over his face. At this distance Hunter could not see what he looked like.

Hurrying back and getting on his own bike Hunter followed, although the man was already out of sight. At Lakeshore Boulevard the tracks showed plainly that the rider had gone to the right. Hunter sped after him.

In a few minutes he felt a thrill. There, not too far ahead, was the man, still crouching over the handlebars as if his very life depended on speed. Hunter pedaled harder, impatient to get a good look at this suspect and see the license number.

Gradually he gained ground. He could see that the man's clothes were all of one piece like a jumpsuit, and splotchy-colored.

Without slowing down, the rider skidded around the hairpin turn at Pine Point. When Hunter made the turn the guy was out of sight around another bend in the road, but Hunter knew there was a mile-long straight stretch a little farther on. He would see the fellow there, and maybe overtake him.

On reaching the straight-away Hunter put on the brakes and stared. Not a soul was in sight. How had the man vanished? Remembering how he and the others had tricked Greg in the woods, Hunter rode slowly on, his keen eyes raking the roadside to see if the man had slipped into the bushes. There wasn't a sign. With a shrug he turned around and set out again for home.

At the Witsoreks' entrance he paused. The man might have ducked in there to avoid him. He scanned the driveway. Yep! A bike had skidded into the lane recently, going fast and spraying loose gravel far and wide.

The boy's heart was pounding as he walked his bike up the private road. He was getting near his man now. He must be careful. When he reached the large rustic house, set in a clearing and surrounded by vegetable and flower garden, he halted. No one was visible. He didn't want to be accused of trespassing, so he went up to the back door. Inside, near the open window, a woman was singing quietly.

At Hunter's knock the singing stopped. The door was opened by an angular middle-aged woman whose hair was knotted at the back of her thin neck. She looked surprised to see a visitor, but she said pleasantly, "Can I help you?"

Hunter's tongue stuck to the roof of his mouth. He wet his lips. "Yes, please, I hope so," he said. "did you happen to see a weird-looking guy ride into your yard a few minutes ago? He was riding a stolen bicycle."

A shocking change came over Miss Witsorek's face. She seemed to turn gray and look much older.

"What makes you say that?" she snapped.

One slim hand fluttered to cover her shaking lips while the other groped for the door and slammed it in Hunter's face.

THE PAINT CLUE

Hunter was so stunned by Miss Witsorek's reaction that for a minute he stood on the doorstep like a carved wooden Indian. Then he picked up his bike and went home.

Back at the cabin he sat down and made a new list in the notebook.

1. Mysterious path to basement door.
2. Door locked inside. No stairs to basement.
3. Green rental stolen from old dock.
4. Fresh green paint here. Used to cover
   ID #?
5. Last night, goofy guy at haunted house.

Can *he* open the locked door? Did he smash my window?

6. Same guy at old house again. Rode off on green bike, *fast*. I followed. He disappeared at Witsorek's.
7. When I asked Miss W. about him, she nearly had a fit and slammed the door.

Absorbed in these tangled threads of mystery, Hunter was startled by a knock on his door. Feeling jittery, he opened it just a crack. There was Greg, looking scared to death.

"What do you want?" Hunter growled.

"I gotta tell ya somethin'."

"I already know you're a spy. A fink," he said.

"Yeah," Greg admitted in a small voice. "But that's not all."

Hunter let him in and stood with arms crossed over his chest, glaring down at the small boy. Greg ran his tongue over his lips. Then words came tumbling out in a rush.

"Kirby's been gambling, and he's up to his neck in debt. He told me that's why he *has* to win the reward quick. He promised me two bucks a day to follow you guys and tell him what you found out."

"That figures," Hunter said. "Go on."

Greg burst out angrily, "Kirby double-crossed me!

Three days I rode my legs off chasing you and Rusty. Now he's mad because I didn't learn nothin'. He won't pay me a cent."

"So?" Hunter demanded.

"I want to get even with him!" Greg cried. "I want to help you find the bikes before he does!"

"Nothing doing," Hunter answered. "You just quit bugging us."

Disappointed, Greg retreated to the porch. There he stopped and with curiosity and awe in his voice asked, "How do you disappear like you done all the time?"

"That's none of your business," the older youth said.

In the morning Rusty almost exploded with excitement over the new developments.

"Was the man on the green bike the clubfoot guy?" he asked.

"No. This guy was wearing army fatigues, and soft shoes. He runs and rides bent over, like he's scared."

"How come you didn't get his license number?"

"The tag was way under the seat and didn't show up."

Rusty had another question. "What kind of folks are the Witsoreks?"

Hunter spoke thoughtfully. "They keep to themselves," he said, "and never make trouble. But . . ." He stopped.

"But what?"

"Well, Miss Witsorek knows *something* . . . and she's scared."

Rusty offered a theory. "Maybe the thief is blackmailing her — or her father — so he can hide on their place!"

Hunter was not impressed. "That kind of thing doesn't happen on Mackinac."

"How do you know?" Rusty answered. "We've got to check every angle. But something seems queer to me. Why would the thief hide bikes so far from town?"

"Yeah," the other agreed. "And how does he plan to get them to the mainland to sell?"

As he spoke, Hunter suddenly saw in his mind's eye the old rotting dock near British Landing. "Say!" he burst out. "Maybe he's taking them away from the dock where we swim!"

"You've got it!" Rusty yelled. "Remember? When we saw the man on Jancy's bike he was headed out this way?"

Hunter frowned. "I kind of think we've got to forget that guy and zero in on this new suspect."

"They might be working together," Rusty guessed.

"Maybe. Anyway, I think we ought to see who has bought spray paint this season."

As they moved off toward the hardware store to do this, Hunter told his partner about Greg's visit. Rusty snorted.

"Serves the kid right," he said. His face grew thoughtful and he added. "I'm glad you turned him down. I bet he's still working for Kirby and was trying to be a double agent."

"Nuts!" Hunter laughed. "You watch too many spy shows on T.V.!"

At the store Hunter got permission to look through the sales slips, saying he had a project to do that involved the sale of paints. The slips were stored in an old shoe box and most of them were written in pencil. Checking them was a slow and boring job. Most paint had been bought in large quantities by hotels and boarding houses. Also by summer people. The first sale of spray paint in small cans had been made to Mr. French.

"Hey!" Rusty cried. "The Beacon Light manager! I'll keep an eye on him."

"He's not stealing bikes," Hunter told him with scorn. "And I used that paint on Saturday, on the fence around the garbage cans."

They continued their search. The only other sale of spray paints had been made to "Ivan Schmitt".

"Who is he?" Rusty asked.

"Never heard of him. But he bought all the right colors."

"What d'ya mean?"

Hunter said, "The notebook shows that all the rentals stolen so far are either red or green or black, and that's exactly what he bought.

"Man!" Rusty exclaimed. "You are something else. I never noticed that. Why do you suppose the thief hasn't stolen bikes of other colors?"

"I don't know . . . but now we've got to track down Mr. Ivan S.!"

They showed the sales slip to the clerk. He didn't know anything about it, so they went to the store manager, Mr. Naughton. He looked at Ivan's name and scratched his bald head.

"I sold the guy the paint but I don't know nothing about him."

"You don't know where he lives or who he works for?"

"No, afraid not."

"Try to remember!" Rusty urged. "We gotta find him."

Mr. Naughton wrinkled his forehead. "I remember I was awful busy. The store was a madhouse. This guy just picked the cans off the shelf and came to the register and paid cash for them."

"What type a guy was he?" Hunter asked.

"He was youngish. Maybe a college student."

A customer called the manager then, so the boys left the store.

"A college student . . ." Hunter was muttering. "I wonder if he's employed somewhere or is just on the island to make easy money stealing bikes. Maybe we should phone all the hotels and ask if he's registered."

"No way!" Rusty exclaimed. "It costs a bundle to stay even at a small place like the Beacon Light. A guy desperate enough to steal bikes wouldn't be in a hotel!"

"Guess you're right," Hunter agreed. "How about boarding houses?"

"That's a better bet," Rusty said. "Where can we go to phone?"

"Have you a phone in your room at the hotel?" Hunter asked.

"Nope." came the answer. "But we could ride out to your place and phone from there."

This struck Hunter as funny. A telephone in Grandfather's cabin! It was only a couple of years ago that the city council had insisted on putting in electricity for the Old Chief! A *telephone*! Keeping his face very sober Hunter folded his arms over his chest, stood as tall and straight as possible, and said with the trace of an accent, "Sorry, Paleface-with-sunset hair, no talking wires in Old Chief's teepee."

Rusty was startled into silence, staring at his friend. Then he burst out laughing and both boys cracked up together. At last Hunter caught his breath and said,

"Maybe we could phone at the library. Let's go and see."

It was only a block to the library. They locked their bikes behind the small building that held the library on the first floor and Mrs. Purcell's apartment up above.

She was delighted to meet Rusty, and eager to hear what they were doing. They told her about the paint clue and asked if she knew Ivan Schmitt.

"I'm afraid not," she said.

"We need to find where he lives, so we can shadow him," said Rusty.

Hunter added, "We want to phone the boarding houses, but I don't even know who runs them."

The librarian smiled. "I've got just what you need — the brochure about places to stay on the island. Complete with telephone numbers. Would you like to use my phone?"

In a few minutes they were at work in her tiny office, making call after call. The results were disappointing. Ivan S. was not registered anywhere. The boys told Mrs. Purcell they didn't know what to do next.

She asked, "Do you have any other clues? Any other suspect?"

"You bet!" Rusty answered. "Hunter, tell her about the bent-over guy."

That was a long story and when Hunter came to the part where Miss Witsorek got so upset and angry, the librarian exclaimed,

"I can't believe it! She's not like that!"

"You know her?" Rusty was amazed.

"I've known her for years. She often comes in to get books for herself and the professor. She's a *nice* person!"

Hunter shrugged. "She must be hiding something or she wouldn't have slammed the door in my face."

Mrs. Purcell shook her gray head. "I can't believe she's involved in any crime," she said firmly. "There's got to be another explanation."

"I think we should go out there now and hunt around for the missing bikes," Rusty suggested.

"We can't," Hunter objected. "If she saw me snooping around I bet she'd call the police."

"Then what do we do?" the redhead demanded. "When and where do we eat? I'm hungry!"

"Me too," Hunter agreed with a grin. "Let's go to Pontiac's Lookout, eat our sandwiches, and then hunt for the hideout. I know dozens of old buildings, empty barns and such, that the thief might use."

"Okay!" Rusty jumped to his feet. "I'm all for that!"

After eating, they spent the afternoon combing the west side of the island for a cache of stolen bikes. It was good they could look forward to supper and the movies, because they had no luck at all. At last they rode down to the Beacon Light. Rusty urged the older boy to stay, but Hunter said he wanted to go home and put on clean things before supper. That gave the redhead a new idea.

"Say," he burst out. "I never thought of it before. How do you manage, about laundry and all that, without a Mom?"

"Easy," Hunter replied. "There's a laundromat here in town. I've used it for years. So long, I'll see ya!"

When Hunter came back to the hotel later, as a guest, he felt awkward at first, and out of place, but Rusty and Mr. Hammergren greeted him warmly. Jancy was already there, wearing a pretty dress and a ribbon in her shining hair.

Mr. Hammergren led the kids at once to the dining room, to a round table by the windows looking out on the lake.

"Ooh, this is neat!" Jancy squealed. "I feel so grown up!"

Laughing, Mr. Hammergren asked, "How old *are* you?"

"I'm a teenager now," she said proudly. "I had a birthday two weeks ago!"

As soon as they were seated Mr. Hammergren said, "We won't have to bother with menus because I've already ordered dinner. I hope you all like steak and French fries, salad and hot rolls!"

The two guests grinned their approval, but Rusty said,

"What? No dessert?"

"You can each choose your own," his Dad promised.

"Way to go!" Rusty cried.

Then Jancy turned eagerly to Hunter. "Rusty said you had an exciting time yesterday, chasing the thief on that green bike! Tell me what happened!"

Hunter's story was so fascinating that when food came Jancy began to eat without even thinking about it. When she heard how Miss Witsorek had shut the door in Hunter's face, she cried,

"Oh, no! What happened then?"

"Nothing. Absolutely nothing," Hunter replied.

Rusty told about the paint clue, and finding Ivan Schmitt's name. That made Jancy sit up and take notice.

"I've seen that name somewhere recently. Since I

came to Mackinac, I think. I wish I could remember where."

They tried to jog her memory, but with no success.

"It's frustrating," Mr. Hammergren admitted. "But don't give up!"

After being quiet a while Jancy said thoughtfully, "I wish I could talk with Miss Witsorek. Maybe I could learn something that would help you."

Rusty laughed. "How in the world could you meet that lady? Even if you did, it would do no good."

"Want to bet!" Jan demanded, with color flooding her face. "I could ride that way tomorrow, and stop in for a drink of water. Mom says I could get a fence post to talk to me!"

"Miss Witsorek is no fence post," Hunter warned her.

With a lift of her chin the new teenager said, "Well, I'd like to try it anyway. You never know what I might discover. And I'll keep looking for that Ivan Schmitt too!"

"Good for you, Jancy!" Mr. Hammergren said. "I think the boys need all the help they can get!"

Hunter was quick to agree. "Yes, we do. So far we have more mysteries than we started with. And no solutions."

As soon as they had finished dinner they walked to

the little movie theater on Market Steet for the early show. A slapstick comedy had them laughing until their sides ached.

It was dark when they came out again. Black storm clouds were racing across the sky. They returned to the hotel for Rusty to get his overnight things and sleeping bag. Then the kids walked their bikes to keep pace with Mr. Hammergren as they all escorted Jancy home.

At the door of Cragmore House Jancy thanked Mr. Hammergren for supper and the movies. Then she added, "Hunter, thanks for this bicycle. Without it I'd have missed all the fun. Rusty, if we go swimming again, I'll teach you to dive without making a flood! And don't be surprised if I help solve the mysteries!"

After goodnights were said, Mr. Hammergren walked downhill alone. The boys rode off toward the center-island road, never guessing what lay ahead.

A VOICE IN THE NIGHT

Soon the boys were in the woods which were unbelievably dark. They rode between the two cemeteries.

Rusty remarked, "You know, Hunter, I never noticed it in the daytime, but at night those gravestones take on queer shapes. It's kinda spooky."

Where the trees met overhead it was so dark they could barely see the road. They got off their bikes and walked. When they came near the Harrisonville crossroad a strange sound came to their ears, halfway between a cry of pain and a grunt. They stopped, puzzled, and tense, straining to identify it. Ahead they could just see a shadowy shape in the road.

Motioning Rusty to stay where he was, Hunter moved forward alone, every sense alert. In a minute he could see that the shape was short, and thick, like a bear. It was uttering weird, husky noises. A chill ran up the boy's spine. Was it an animal? Or a man? He inched closer until a mixture of smells reached his nose. Tobacco and liquor. At the same time he began to make out words, in a familiar voice. Hunter's heart sank but he beckoned to Rusty.

"It's okay," he said in a hoarse whisper. "It's — it's my Dad."

Timber Martineau stared at the boys stupidly. "I was going to the cabin to find you, Hunter," he mumbled.

"What's the matter, Dad?" Hunter asked.

It was like a knife in the boy's heart to have Rusty see his father like this. He swallowed hard.

"My leg," Tim complained. "There's a storm coming and my leg hurts something fierce. I quit early and I know I can't do no work tomorrow."

Hunter understood. This had happened over and over again. Bad weather made the old injury painful and his father went to the bar for relief.

Tim muttered, "I'll lose my job. You gotta live with us and help me."

His pathetic voice faded while Hunter was thinking what to do. Setting his kickstand, he went to Tim and placed his hands on the broad shoulders, turning his father back toward the village and speaking quietly.

"I'll help you all I can, Dad," he said. "but I have to live in the cabin. You go home now. Bella will give you some coffee, and you'll feel better."

Obediently Tim started to go, then something seemed to penetrate the fog in his mind. He straightened up. Thrusting his shaggy head close to Hunter's face his words came out in a roar.

"Who do you think you are, telling me what to do?" he demanded. "And what are you doing out here at midnight? Who's that punk with you and what trouble have you been up to?"

Hunter's stomach churned in anger and misery.

"It's all right, Dad," he answered.

"All right?" Tim burst out roughly. "It's all wrong. You're my son and you'll have to live where I can keep an eye on you!"

"Look, Dad," Hunter said, "this is my friend Rusty. His Dad took us to the movies and now he's coming back to spend the night with me."

In a minute or two Tim quieted again, and soon shuffled off toward the village, his limp more noticeable than usual.

The boys went on their way without a word until Rusty heard a far-off sound.

"Is that a dog barking?" he asked.

"No," said Hunter, "that's a great horned owl."

He tipped his head back, cupped both hands over his mouth and sent out a throaty call.

"Hoo, hoohoo, hoo hoo."

Before long there came an answer, nearer this time.

"Hoo, hoohoo, hoo hoo."

"Man-oh-man," Rusty whispered. "Your call was so real it fooled him!"

When they reached the cabin Hunter got out milk and cookies. By the soft light of the kerosene lamp, the boys talked before going to bed. Hunter was glad Rusty said nothing about what had happened at the crossroads.

He told Rusty to spread his sleeping bag on the Old Chief's bed. After blowing out the lamp he went to his bunk in the other room.

Hours later the wail of a siren right outside the cabin woke him. Hunter sat up with a jerk. A fire siren? Here? He must have been dreaming.

"What's that?" Rusty called.

Hunter switched on the light, opened the front door and looked out. The strident noise had died away. There was nothing unusual to be seen. Of course not. Hunter closed the door and perched on

Grandfather's bed. He and Rusty stared at each other. A fire siren screaming *here*! Yet they both heard it.

"This is more kooky than I bargained for," Rusty said in a whisper.

While they were still dazed a voice reached them through the back window, which was open.

"Listen to me, my son. Listen and obey."

Hunter gripped Rusty's arm like a vise. "It's Grandfather!" he breathed.

"Listen to me, Hunter!" the quavering voice of the old man went on. "You must leave the cabin and live with your people. Hunter, obey me!"

The boys waited. The Big Ben on the shelf ticked loudly. There was no other sound indoors or out. Finally Hunter picked up a flashlight.

"Come on, Rusty. Let's take a look outside."

Sticking close together the boys circled the house, shining the light in every direction. They looked behind the woodpile and the trees. Even up in the branches. No one was there. Thunder grumbled in the distance and lightning flashed, adding to the weirdness of the hour.

When they went in, Rusty asked in a voice full of awe, "Did it really sound like the Old Chief?"

"It was Grandfather's voice," Hunter said. "No doubt about it. But . . ."

"But what?"

"One thing puzzles me."

"What's that?"

"Well," Hunter answered slowly. "Most of the time Grandfather called me 'son'. But when he wanted to impress something on my mind he used the name he gave me at my name-ceremony."

In a whisper Rusty asked, "What's that?"

"He called me 'Mighty Hunter'."

Rusty's mouth opened but he said nothing. Hunter thinking aloud, went on.

"If Grandfather wanted me to pay attention and obey, he would have said 'Mighty Hunter'. I'm sure of it."

The boys talked in hushed voices for quite a while. About the siren and the voice. They could not explain those mysteries no matter how hard they tried.

"I'm glad you are here, and heard it too," Hunter said. "Otherwise I'd be sure I dreamed it."

Then the storm struck. Rain poured down in a flood. Lightning made the boys blink, and thunder shook the snug cabin.

"Heck!" Hunter said when he could make himself heard. "This will wash away any signs I might have seen outdoors in the morning."

He was right. Even in the bright sunshine of a beautiful fresh day he could not find a single clue that anyone or anything had been near the cabin in the night.

"I don't know what to do," Hunter said. "If Grandfather told me to live with Dad, I would move. But he didn't like me to spend time in the village. He was afraid I'd lose my Indian ways. Like Dad."

Later he said with some hesitation, "Rusty, you told me you did a project on Indians at school. Did you ever come across the idea of a 'guiding dream'?"

"Yeah, but I don't remember much about it. Why?"

"Do you think a guiding dream might help me decide about moving?"

"That's a cool idea! How do you do it?"

"First you have to go without any food for at least one day. Then you go off by yourself, pick the right place, and sleep. Your dream tells you what to do, or you see something that points the right way. I sure need help. Where to live, and how to return the bi — "

He stopped himself just before saying 'binoculars'.

Rusty was excited. "You haven't had breakfast yet. You could fast today and have the dream tomorrow!"

"But I'm supposed to look after you," Hunter objected.

"Nuts!" the redhead said. "I can look after myself. And I've got to get souvenirs for Mom and my sis."

"A dream might take all day," Hunter warned.

"No problem," Rusty grinned. "In the afternoon I'll take Jancy sketching. How do you know where to have your dream?"

"Well," came the answer. "Old time Indians believed their totem would show them the right place. My totem is the owl, but I don't know how — "

"Hey!" Rusty interrupted. "Speaking of owls, where is the owl headdress you told me about? So much happened last night I forgot all about the treasures. Where are they?"

Hunter answered, "After the window was smashed, I hid them. See if you can find them. While you're doing that I'll make your breakfast and fix your sandwiches for lunch. I won't eat."

Hunter enjoyed the next twenty minutes. He watched Rusty searching high and low, in drawers and under the beds. He even looked in the pot-bellied stove and outside under the porch.

At last he said, "I bet you buried them."

"Well sort of," Hunter admitted. "If you'll swear not to tell a soul, I'll show you."

Rusty made the vow and crossed his heart.

Out of the woodbox came the wood. Then Hunter lifted out the odd, bulky bundles. Rusty swung a straight chair around and sat on it with his arms resting on its back. His face was glowing with interest. Hunter laid the feathered headdress on the bed.

118

Shaking his head in amazement Rusty said, "I've seen an eagle headdress in the museum, but never one like this. How come it's made like an owl?"

"I told you," Hunter answered, "my family belongs to the owl clan, so — "

"I didn't know Indians had clans as well as tribes," Rusty cut in.

"Sure. The Ottawas had lots of clans, named for a wild creature that was their totem. Pontiac's was the otter. He signed his birchbark messages with the otter's paw-mark."

Rusty's eyes were round with wonder. "How come you know a thing like that?" he asked.

"Grandfather told me," Hunter said. He paused and then continued. "You see, Pontiac was a far-off grandfather of mine."

Rusty stared at his friend. "He was? Geeee!" Then he remarked, "You said Pontiac's totem was the otter. How come yours is the owl?"

Hunter explained that he was related through one of Pontiac's granddaughters who had married a man in the owl clan. Ottawa families always took the totem of the father.

Rusty made Hunter wear the headdress while he unwrapped the rest of the artifacts. The mainland boy was fascinated with each item and pumped his friend for all the Indian lore he could get.

The morning was almost gone when at last they put the priceless objects away. Hunter said the next thing to do was to check out some empty buildings he had remembered last night just before going to sleep. It was property called Silver Birches on the East Shore Boulevard a little beyond Pine Point. Rusty loaded his things on his bike and the boys set out. They passed the Witsorek entrance and were soon at Silver Birches.

It had been a kind of camp. There were two cottages and a dormitory-type building, all unused for years. They were handy to the road and would have been a good place for the stolen bicycles. The boys looked carefully through every window they could reach, but once more came up empty-handed.

It was lunch time so they went down beside the lake. While Rusty ate his sandwiches Hunter skipped rocks, trying to convince himself he wasn't hungry.

When Rusty had finished he said to Hunter, "I'd like to know more about Pontiac. Could I get a book from the library?"

"Sure," said Hunter. "We'll go there now."

Mrs. Purcell was glad to help. She picked out the best book on the great chief, and signed it out on Hunter's card.

Back again on the street they saw Kirby, who was collecting trash. He put a friendly hand on Hunter's shoulder.

"Say, boy, you don't look so good. Is something bothering you?"

Hunter thought about his empty stomach, the siren, and the voice in the night, but he shook his head.

"Are you about ready to leave the cabin?" the trashman asked with concern.

"N-no," Hunter said. "I haven't quite made up my mind yet."

"Well, let me know when you do," Kirby reassured him. "I'm ready to help you, even if we are competing for those rewards! You may decide to move sooner than you think."

Kirby drove on down the street. When he was out of hearing, Rusty asked, "What did he mean by that?"

"I haven't a clue," Hunter answered.

BLACKMAIL

From the library the boys went to the Beacon Light to leave Rusty's things. As they came out they met his father coming in.

"What luck!" he said. "I wanted to see you, Rusty."

"How come?"

"A bunch of us are making a quick trip to Sault Ste. Marie to see the famous Soo Locks. Want to along?"

"You bet!" Rusty answered. "Is that okay with you, Hunter?"

"Sure," Hunter said. "You ought to see 'em."

When the Hammergrens headed for the ferry dock, Hunter went to the police booth. He wanted more details about the bike stolen the day before. With those in his notebook, he asked if any bikes had disappeared today.

"No," the officer answered. "Not yet."

Hunter started home on the center-island road. By now he was so hungry he wondered how the old-time Indians had managed to fast three days before a guiding dream. He hoped his dream would be worth this growling, painful stomach.

As he turned into the trail to the cabin he was startled to see a man hurrying toward him. It was Kirby Tyson, carrying something in a brown paper bag. Dropping his bike, Hunter blocked the path. When Kirby saw Hunter, he jumped, tucked his package under one arm and lit a cigarette.

"What have you got in that bag?" Hunter demanded.

The trashman raised his eyebrows. "Nothing of yours," he declared. "I am not a thief, like a certain guy I could name."

"Well, why are you here?" Hunter asked.

"As a matter of fact I came to ask you a favor. I need money bad, so bad I'm doing a second job, at night, on the quiet. I'm painting furniture for a man who is away," he went on. "I've run out of paint for the porch chairs and I can't get more myself. You see, Mr. Naughton, in the store, is on the city council. If he finds out I'm moonlighting, I could lose my trash job."

Kirby paused and blew out a cloud of smoke. As Hunter waited to hear more, he realized the dray had not been on the road. How had Kirby come from downtown?

The trashman went on. 'I'll give you money to buy me a can of green spray paint," he said.

Hunter's face was a mask, hiding sudden excitement. Green spray paint! *Could Kirby be the bike thief?* Common sense calmed him. No way! Kirby worked all day. Besides, if he were the thief, he wouldn't have hired Greg to spy for him.

Kirby, holding the cigarette with his lips, dug a couple of bills out of his pocket.

"Here's the dough," he said.

"Forget it!" Hunter snapped the words at him. "I want to know why you were at the cabin and what's in your bag."

"That's none of your business," Kirby answered. "Here, take the money and get the paint. Quick."

"I won't do it!" Hunter said, putting his hands behind his back.

To his astonishment the trashman's expression changed. Instead of getting angrier he looked pleased. His thin lips smiled.

"Oh yes you will!" he replied.

"I will not!" Hunter answered through clenched teeth. Kirby might knock him down, but he would *not* do the man's errand.

Kirby, without even raising his fists, delivered a crushing blow. "If you don't do what I say," he announced, "I'll tell Mr. Clemson you have his binocs!"

Hunter was stunned. Dizzy. This couldn't be happening. It was gross. He wanted to tell Kirby he had only borrowed the glasses, but he couldn't get the words out. His mind worked frantically, seeking some way out this trap. He was helpless as a fox caught in sharp steel jaws.

Kirby waited, grinning. He was clearly enjoying his power. At last Hunter reached out and took the money.

"Leave the paint and the change in a sack behind the library," Kirby directed him. "And remember. Don't let anyone know it's for me."

"Okay," the boy muttered. Then he flung up his head and challenged the trashman. "Before I do that I'm going to the cabin and check out things there!"

Kirby shrugged. "Go right ahead!" he said.

Hunter wheeled his bike along the path, wondering again how Kirby got there. His bike had not been in sight on the road.

The cabin looked all right and the door was locked. Inside, everything was in order; the woodbox had not been touched. That was a relief. Outside, behind the house, things were different. The ground by the wood-pile, damp from last night's storm, was all churned up with bootprints. It looked as if the wood had been spilled and then re-piled. Yep. Some of the sticks were muddy. What in the world had Kirby been looking for? What had he found?

As Hunter studied the ground he got another shock. In several places he saw a bootprint he recognized. A thrill of discovery ran up his spine. There was the same mark he had found after the window was smashed. One corner of the heel was missing! So Kirby had thrown that rock! Why had he done that? What was he up to this time? Had Kirby hidden some dangerous device in the woodpile?

That was hard to believe. Still, Hunter took time for a brief inspection. He found nothing suspicious. Starving, he started inside, to make a sandwich. Just in time he remembered that he must not eat. He locked up and rode down the trail.

Hunter was going at a good clip when he reached the road. He was annoyed to see that Kirby was still there, near the old house. Without a word, Hunter turned downhill to take the shore route to town. Kirby yelled at him to go the other way, but Hunter paid no attention. He pedaled faster.

Hitting the paved road at high speed he took the

corner with a squealing skid and ran right into a vehicle that had been hidden by the trees. It happened so fast all Hunter knew was that he hit his head and twisted one leg. He and the bicycle fell in a heap.

He lay quiet for a minute or two. Then slowly he sat up, wondering what had happened. He felt his head. There was a lump above one eye but no blood. When he moved his leg it hurt, but it wasn't broken. Pulling himself to his feet Hunter saw it was the trash wagon he had run into. The sleepy team was tied to the historic marker. Although he was dazed, it wasn't long before the boy realized he had an answer to one of his questions. Kirby had come on the dray, and then walked up the hill to the cabin.

Anger against the trashman flamed up in him. It grew as he noticed that Kirby had allowed papers to blow out of the wagon and across the road. From force of habit Hunter began to pick up the scattered trash. One piece had blown into the woods. When Hunter lifted it he saw a bicycle license tag on the ground. Picking it up, he noted the number — 629 — and wondered how it got there. Pulling out his notebook and making a quick check, he saw that none of the missing bikes had had that number. It might be a clue, or it might not. He straightened the handlebars of his bike and mounted. He was so full of this new discovery he paid no attention to his sore leg.

When he got to town he bought the paint for Kirby and left it as directed. The police station was only a short distance away, so he took the license tag to the officer on duty. That man looked at it and then jumped up as if he had been bitten on the seat.

"Hey!" he shouted. "This is from a black bike stolen only an hour or so ago! Where did you find it?"

"Where the center road joins the lakeshore," Hunter answered. "Where was it stolen from?"

"At Devil's Kitchen," said the policeman. "A tourist was in the cave hunting for ancient Indian drawings on the walls. When he came out, no bike."

"Thanks!" Hunter called as he ran out the door.

He leaped on his bike, riding back the way he had just come. The wheels in his head were turning as fast as the ones on his bicycle.

The thief must have been walking by Devil's Kitchen when he saw an easy chance to take a bike. One squirt of black paint and the ID number was gone. Then he could ride to his hideout and no one would suspect him.

A new thought struck the boy. Why had the thief thrown away the license? That didn't make sense at all. At this point he had a memory flashback. He remembered when he and Rusty had watched Kirby at Sugar Loaf. Kirby had picked up the photographer's bike, and Rusty had thought he was going to put it in the dray. He hadn't. But maybe he had done that very thing today.

It dawned on Hunter that Kirby, on his way from downtown had driven past Devil's Kitchen. He could easily have put the bike in the wagon, covering it with trash and tarp. At the marker he might have stopped to get rid of the metal license tag.

Another fact pointed to Kirby as a possible thief. More green bikes had vanished than any other color, and it was that color he had run out of . . .

One fact was still a puzzle. Why had Kirby left the dray and *walked* uphill and on to the cabin? What had he been doing at the woodpile when he had knocked it over?

These questions were still bothering Hunter when he reached Devil's Kitchen. He stopped by the litter cans. Often they were overflowing with trash because this was a favorite picnic spot. Both were empty. That proved Kirby had been at the scene of the theft at the right time!

Hunter sped along, hoping the dray would still be at the marker. It was gone, but he saw its tire treads going up the center road. He followed. The dray had not stopped at the haunted house and Hunter did not stop either.

Half a mile farther on, the tire-marks turned left onto a secondary road. Left again onto the narrow dirt track to the landfill. Hunter's hopes rose. He was on the right trail for sure. Maybe he could catch Kirby unloading the black bike.

He rounded a bend and came nose to nose with the two big horses. Kirby was not in sight and the wagon was empty.

"Heck!" Hunter exclaimed. "I'm too late."

He decided to hide until the trashman drove away. Then he would search the area. Before he could do this, Kirby came from the trees and saw him. There was no use in running away. Hunter waited.

"Did you put the paint where I told you?" Kirby asked.

The boy nodded, and Kirby went on. "The next thing I want you to do," he announced, "is to move out of the cabin. Today."

Hunter could have not been more surprised and upset if Kirby had pulled the ground out from under his bicycle.

"Wh-what?" he stammered. "Why?"

"Never mind why," the man answered. "Starting tonight you live at your Dad's house. I'm next door. I'll check up on you."

"Where I live is none of your business," Hunter said.

"Either you sleep in the village tonight, or in jail,"

Kirby told him. "I'll tell the police about the binoculars, and that will fix you."

Kirby climbed to his seat and drove off, calling over his shoulder, "Take what you need for tonight. We'll get the rest of your junk later."

Hunter's empty stomach was tied in a knot. His head was splitting, and his leg hurt. He didn't know if he could ride, or even walk.

THE SECRET ENTRANCE

Hunter did not move a muscle until the dray had disappeared. Then he let the bicycle fall. He limped slowly to a big tree and sat down against it. One fact numbed his brain: if Kirby could make him move, he could make him do anything.

This was the end, just when he had thought victory was in sight. If only he could ask Grandfather what to do. He knew the Old Chief wouldn't want him to give in to Kirby without a fight, but what weapons could he use against blackmail?

His thoughts drifted again to the bike that had vanished today. He had jumped to the conclusion that Kirby took it, but he had no proof. If he did steal the bike, where had he put it? Maybe there was a shed near the dump. If so, Kirby could hide his loot when he emptied the dray. Perhaps he had just done that.

Aching and hungry though he was, Hunter made himself get up and search. The hideout must be near, and there should be a path worn to it. Although he looked carefully he found no path, no shed. He started home, feeling he had been wrong in branding Kirby as the thief. Apparently he had not picked up the bicycle at the Devil's Kitchen. Maybe the guy in the jumpsuit was the real thief after all. Perhaps *he* had torn off the license and tossed it away as he rode toward the Witsorek place.

At home Hunter drank a glass of milk and lay on his bed. He wanted to sleep and forget his troubles, but he couldn't. Finally he got up, rolled up his sleeping bag, and stuffed his pajamas and toothbrush into his knapsack. He thought about the artifacts and the binoculars, deciding to leave them where they were.

Hunter puzzled again why Kirby was so determined to make him move. There was a missing link somewhere. Did the trashman want to use the cabin? For a gambling spot, maybe?

The more Hunter thought about leaving the cabin, the more he rebelled. He felt keenly it was important for him to go to his guiding dream straight from

Grandfather's house. He refused to let a creep like Kirby foul that up.

The Big Ben ticked off minute after minute as Hunter wrestled with his problem. At last he relaxed and smiled. He had figured out a way to fool the trashman.

Just before sunset Hunter put on his knapsack and rode his loaded bicycle to the village. He left it leaning against his Dad's house on the side next to Kirby's, where the trashman would be sure to see it.

Taking his things inside, Hunter dropped them behind a chair and joined the family watching TV. Little Sam was asleep in the old baby carriage that was his bed. About ten o'clock Bella took the girls off to bed. That gave Hunter a chance to talk with his father.

"Dad," he said, "I've been fasting so I can seek a guiding dream tomorrow. I'm going back to the cabin, but I want *everyone* to think I spent the night here."

"What for?" Tim Martineau asked.

"Dad, I — I can't tell you now. But I need your help."

Timber looked very solemn as he said, "Son, I can't help you if I don't know what the trouble is. How about a man–to–man talk?"

Hunter hesitated. Would his father understand?

"N — not yet, Dad," he said at last. "Maybe . . . after the dream."

"Well, what do you want me to do?"

"I'll leave my sleeping bag here, like I slept in it, with my pj's and stuff," Hunter answered. "In the morning, will you just let the family think I got up and went out early?"

Tim said it sounded crazy to him, but he'd do it. So, after everyone was in bed and the house was dark, Hunter slung the empty knapsack on one shoulder and slipped like a shadow out the back door. There were no street lights in Harrisonville. He was sure he could not be seen from the Tyson house. He set out on foot.

At the cabin he let himself in and relocked the door. He didn't turn on the light, but settled himself cross-legged on Grandfather's bed. In the darkness he could pretend the Old Chief was in his chair, ready to listen and help.

In a low voice Hunter poured out the story of the binoculars, and Kirby's blackmail. What should he do? There was no voice answering him but Hunter felt his Grandfather did not like the set-up at all. He knew the old man would tell him to give back the glasses. That was impossible. There was no way.

Next Hunter spoke about leaving the cabin.

"It was so strange," he whispered, "when the siren

woke me up and I heard your voice. *Was* it you, Grandfather? Do you really want me to live in the village?"

To these questions there was no answer at all.

Hunter began to think of other things. Why did he see Kirby around here so often lately? *Was* he the thief? Who had worn the path to the basement door of the old house? And *how* did he get in?

In his mind Hunter started searching the house inch by inch, hunting for some way to the basement. After several minutes, like a flash of lightning, it came to him. It was so obvious he should have thought of it before. There must be a trapdoor somewhere!

Hunter leaped to his feet. He couldn't wait to see if he was right. So what if it was the middle of the night!

Taking his flashlight the boy went out into the darkness. He raced down the familiar trail. At the road the ancient house loomed black and ghostly against the star-lit sky but Hunter never hesitated. With the light in one hand he climbed in the broken window.

Shoving the furniture off the rug, he flung back one corner of it and let out a war-whoop. Under the rug was a neat trapdoor with an inset handle. He hooked his finger into the ring and pulled.

The trapdoor opened easily. It revealed a ladder going into a black hole that was the basement. With his heart beating fast, Hunter put his feet on the rungs and started going down. The ladder wobbled and slid sideways. Hunter, quickly grabbing the edge of the opening, steadied it, but the flashlight slipped out of his hand. It landed below with a thud and went out. The blackness was like a thick blanket around him. He stayed still, trying to control the shaking of his body.

The ladder was still in place. In a minute, holding on with both hands and moving cautiously, Hunter went down into the inky dark. When at last his feet were on the ground he paused for breath. If he left the ladder, to hunt for the flashlight, he might have trouble finding it again. He might even knock the ladder over and be unable to put it back in place until morning light. He kneeled down with his left hand on the bottom rung and swept his other hand in a circle over the hard-packed earth floor, and found nothing. A second, larger sweep was also unsuccessful. On the third sweep his hand hit the flashlight and he carefully picked it up, thinking, "What good will it do me, if the bulb is broken?"

He pressed the switch and magically, marvelously the light came on! Hunter stood up. Swinging the light triumphantly he looked around the basement. He lost his breath as completely as if he had fallen with the ladder on top of him.

The basement was full of bicycles. Red, green, and black bicycles without any identification.

"Wahoo!" he shouted, when he had caught his breath. "Wait till I tell Rusty! I never dreamed the bikes were *here!*"

He turned his light on the door to the backyard. It was fastened with a hasp and a padlock. He thought a minute until he figured out how the thief must operate this unsuspected hideout. Apparently he rode each bike to the door at the back. That explained the path from the road. Leaving the bike there, he went into the house and down the ladder. Opening the door, he brought the bike in, and snapped the padlock shut again. Then up the ladder he went, covered the trapdoor with the rug, and put the furniture and trash back as before. All this took less than five minutes, Hunter guessed, and probably the thief came at night when tourist traffic was rare.

Hunter went up the ladder and hid the secret entrance just as the thief had done. He crawled out the window and sat on the edge of the porch a few minutes, tingling with the excitement of his discovery. He had found the missing bikes! He had earned fifty bucks! Now — what about catching the thief too?

That would be easy now. He and Rusty could leave their bikes at the cabin, hide in the haunted house — maybe on the second floor so they wouldn't be seen. They would wait for the thief to bring his latest bicycle and get a good description of him to give to the police.

Would it be the handicapped man, or the person Miss Witsorek was protecting? Would it be someone else? Or — could it be Kirby Tyson, after all?

Suddenly Hunter knew it *had* to be Kirby. Several facts pointed to the trashman.

He must have picked up that bike at Devil's Kitchen yesterday and unloaded it here before going on to the dump. The same thing must have happened Monday with the kid's bike stolen at the old dock. After spraying the ID number, Kirby could have slipped the rental under the tarp and brought it here. Yes! Hunter remembered now meeting the empty dray when he was trying to catch up with the thief.

He recalled something else. Kirby didn't drive the trash wagon on Sundays, so of course no bikes disappeared! The riddle of Sundays was solved, almost proving Kirby was the thief. All his talk about looking for the bikes and doing a second job was just cover-up. Hey! Kirby got Greg to tail him and Rusty so he would know if they were hot on his trail!

Hunter jumped down from the porch and did a victory dance. He started toward the cabin bursting with excitement and pride.

As he opened the door, a forgotten fact hit him. If

Kirby *was* the thief, Hunter could not report him to the police. He could not win the rewards, or Kirby would turn *him* over to the police too. It was as simple and clear as that.

"Why, oh why, did the thief have to be Kirby?"

Even a guiding dream could not change these facts.

THE GUIDING DREAM

Faced with Kirby's power over him, Hunter paced back and forth in the dark cabin. The hours dragged by. Gradually the black rectangle of the window faded to gray, and finally light came. Brilliant sunshine made the outdoor world new, but none of that brightness reached Hunter's heart.

Why bother about a guiding dream now? Still, having set his mind on it, he decided to go ahead. Maybe the dream would help him face the future.

As he got ready to leave he did two things he hadn't planned. Putting his loafers into his knapsack, he slid his feet into Grandfather's moccasins. Then he went to the cedar tree, got the binoculars, and put them in with the loafers. He had no reason for doing this. He just felt he must not leave the glasses behind. Then an idea came. Perhaps he would need them to see a bird that would be part of the message of his dream.

There were miles of foot-trails on Mackinac and Hunter knew them well. He followed one after another without any clear idea where he meant to go. Maybe the moccasins were choosing his path. After an hour or so he came to a high out-cropping of rock in the middle of the island called Point Lookout. Below him was Sugar Loaf, the teepee made of rock, the home of the Great Spirit. Yes! That was the place for his dream.

Going down through the woods, Hunter was soon on a level with the road. He slipped from tree to tree until he found a little hollow like a hammock. It was screened by bushes and carpeted with pine needles. The sounds of tourists seemed to come from a different world. Lying there on his back, Hunter could see the top of the "teepee" against the blue sky. The first thing he noticed was a fluffy white cloud sailing by. It had the shape of a great horned owl. His totem. It was a sign he had reached the right spot. For the first time since Kirby's blackmailing began, Hunter relaxed and was instantly asleep.

It was the sharp snapping of a dead twig, hours

later, that finally woke him. He opened his eyes, stared, closed them in disbelief, opened them again.

Gazing down at him was an old, old Indian chief, dressed in fringed buckskins. The chief wore a brown furry headdress with buffalo horns on it. His face was like ancient tanned leather, furrowed with wrinkles. On his broad chest were many strings of beads. His hands were in white buckskin gloves, and he held a strange, carved stick. These details and many more were imprinted on Hunter's memory in one look. But his eyes were drawn back to the bronzed face.

Although he felt awake, Hunter knew this must be a dream. No Indian like this had ever lived on Mackinac. Or, *had He*? Had the great teepee been His home ages and ages ago?

"What is your name, my son, and why are you sleeping here in the shadow of the Great Spirit's home?" the old Indian asked in a rich, low voice.

"My name is Hunter Martineau. I do not know what to do, so I am seeking a guiding dream," the boy answered.

"Tell me what troubles you."

Hunter spoke first about the Old Chief, who had made him proud to be an Indian. "Now he is gone. People tell me to live in the village. I want to stay in Grandfather's cabin. I need to guard the Indian treasures he left in my care. But that is not all."

Hunter went on to tell about taking the binoculars, and finding the stolen bicycles, and how he hated Kirby for blackmailing him.

"You are the Great Spirit," he said at last. "You can tell me what I should do."

The ancient Indian face creased even more as the chief smiled. He spoke slowly.

"I am not the Great Spirit," he said, "only one of His sons like you. I came to this sacred island to learn more of His wisdom. I know the temptation to hate. But that is not the Great Spirit's way. He sends the sun and rain on all His sons of every color, the good and the bad."

"Who *are* you?" Hunter asked.

"I am Walking Buffalo, chief of the Stony Tribe of Western Canada. For ninety years I have been learning from the Great Spirit, so perhaps I can help you."

The chief raised his leathery face to the sky.

"I have found," he said, "that when His sons listen to Him, He plants in the heart one thought, one command. When that is obeyed, He reveals the next step. Tell me, is there any one thing you know He wants you to do?"

Very low, Hunter answered, "I know I should give the glasses back to my teacher. But what if he turns me over to the police?"

Chief Walking Buffalo looked at the boy's feet, and

smiled. "You have already chosen to walk in your grandfather's moccasins. Place them on the path the Great Spirit shows you. The next step will be clear. Then the next. And the next. You will become a mighty Hunter."

Hunter looked up with awe into the dark eyes that had narrowed to tiny slits as the chief smiled.

"I will do it," the boy said. "But how did you know Grandfather named me 'Mighty Hunter'?"

The only answer was a deepening of the chief's smile.

After a pause Hunter asked, "Shall I move, or stay in the cabin?"

"Obey your heart, my son. When the time comes to decide, you will know what is right. Now, close your eyes and let the Great Spirit breathe His peace into your mind and body."

Hunter obeyed, drawing in great gulps of the cedar-scented air. He felt at peace. He slept again.

When he woke it was late afternoon and the sun was low. He was alone. Sitting up and stretching, Hunter wondered, "Was it all a dream? It seemed so real!"

The next minute he knew it had been no dream. Beside him lay the strange ceremonial stick Chief Walking Buffalo had carried. Hunter's fingers closed around it with a thrill of pleasure. The chief had left it for him. An Indian treasure of his very own. Hunter rose to his feet, eager to be on his way and do what he had promised.

Because he was hurrying, the moccasins kept slipping off his feet. He paused long enough to change to his loafers.

As he strode along, heedless of the tourists around him, he thought about Mr. Clemson. He was nothing special to look at, but he was easily the best-loved teacher on the island. Mr. Clemson was of medium height, and trim. He had mousy hair that crinkled in waves across his head. Beside a rather flat nose his eyes were usually warm and kind. Hunter knew, though, that when the teacher was fired up to fight for something he believed in, those eyes could darken and seem to shoot sparks.

Hunter had often felt Mr. Clemson pulling for him, even though he sometimes skipped school and didn't care about good grades. Mr. Clemson was a great guy to have on your side. What would it be like to have those honest eyes shooting sparks at you? His heart sank as he realized he would lose the teacher's respect when he admitted being a thief.

Mr. Clemson's house, which he shared with another Mackinac teacher, was on a side street off Market Street, and was almost hidden by trees. As Hunter knocked on the door he was suddenly afraid. He might be behind bars tonight. A glance at Chief Walking Buffalo's staff renewed his courage. He stood tall.

Mr. Clemson welcomed the boy with a smile. The binoculars were still in the knapsack. Wasting no time Hunter took them out and held them toward the man.

"I took them from your desk," he said. "I'm sorry. I won't ever do a thing like that again."

Mr. Clemson's expression did not change. He accepted the glasses, looking keenly into Hunter's face. The boy did not drop his eyes.

"Come in," the teacher said, leading the way to his small kitchen. "Come in and sit down."

Hunter, tense as a bow string, perched on the edge of a chair. In his normal voice Mr. Clemson asked,

"Would you like some milk and cookies while we talk?"

Hunter let go his reserve. "You bet!" he exclaimed. "I haven't had anything to eat since day before yesterday!"

"*What*?" Mr. Clemson said, showing more surprise than when Hunter returned the binoculars. "Why not?"

While his teacher got out bread, peanut butter, and jelly, as well as milk and cookies, Hunter told the reasons for his fasting and dream — the binoculars, the bicycles in the old house, everything. He wound up by saying,

"Kirby just has to be the thief, but I couldn't report him, or I'd go to jail too."

Mr. Clemson's homely face broke into a beaming smile.

"But now," he said. "Kirby can't do a thing to you. You had the guts to put right what was wrong, so you are a free man again!"

"You aren't going to turn me in?" Hunter asked.

The teacher's eyebrows shot up the way they did in school when some kid asked a dumb question.

"There's no need. You've learned your lesson."

Hunter felt like a helium balloon taking off into the blue. When he touched earth again he asked Mr. Clemson how he thought Chief Walking Buffalo happened to be on the spot when Hunter needed him. Thinking it over, the teacher said, "I'm sure he came to Mackinac for an inter-racial conference at one of the hotels. I guess it was his own closeness to the Great Spirit that led him to you."

Hunter nodded. That made sense.

"What are you going to do next about the stolen bikes?" Mr. Clemson asked.

"Tomorrow Rusty and I will hide in the old house and identify the thief. Then we'll report him to the police. Say," he broke off. "What day is this?"

Mr. Clemson said, "Thursday. Why?"

"Geee —" distressed, Hunter let out a long breath.

"Rusty goes home Friday. What a shame for him to miss the fun!"

"Maybe you could get his father to stay one more day," the teacher suggested.

"Yeah!" Hunter agreed. "We'll try anyway, tonight. I can't wait to see Kirby's face when he's arrested."

Mr. Clemson grinned like a boy. "I'd like to see *your* face if Kirby isn't the thief!" Then he grew serious. "Listen, Hunter, don't you and Rusty take any chances. That thief will be desperate, and maybe dangerous."

"We'll be careful," Hunter promised, getting up to go. "And thanks, Mr. Clemson. For everything!"

RUSTY AND JAN DISAPPEAR

Hunter wanted to go straight to the Beacon Light, but he thought he might hit the Hammergrens' supper time. He decided to go first to the village and get his bike. He left the precious staff at Dad's house, hidden on a shelf. Then he rode back to town.

Mr. Hammergren was on the hotel porch looking annoyed.

"Hunter!" he called out. "Do you know where Rusty is?"

"He's not here?" Hunter asked in amazement.

"No, he's not, and it's way past supper time."

"I'm sure he meant to be back by now," Hunter

150

said. "He was going to take Jancy sketching. Maybe she made him late. Or he might be at her house."

"I'll phone and find out," Mr. Hammergren said. "Wait here, will you?"

Hunter chuckled to himself. Maybe Jancy wanted to finish a sketch, and now Rusty was going to catch it! Suddenly he remembered the girl's idea of dropping in at Miss Witsorek's to ask for a drink, and talk to the lady. Had something gone wrong there?

When Mr. Hammergren came back his frown had deepened.

"They have not come home and Mrs. DuPont is worried. She's afraid they went swimming and had an accident."

Hunter was silent, thinking things over. It was not like Rusty to lose track of time.

"I'm not worried," Rusty's Dad said, "but I'd like to tan Rusty's hide for being so irresponsible."

"I'll go and find them if you like," Hunter offered.

"Would you? That would be great. I feel so help-less without a car, or even a bike!"

If the kids *had* gone swimming, or had called on Miss Witsorek, Hunter figured, they would ride home by Arch Rock, the quickest way. He rode off past Marquette Park and Island House, sure he would meet them speeding homeward. But they didn't show up. He rounded Robinson's Folly and reached Arch Rock.

151

Still no sign of the two. Well, there was nothing to do but keep going.

The road was almost empty of tourists at this time of day. Just as he was nearing the Witsorek place he saw in the distance a familiar figure coming toward him. It was a man bent over, pedaling madly, and he had a cap pulled down over his face.

Thoughts of his missing friends flew out of Hunter's mind like leaves before a hurricane. This was too good a chance to miss. He put on his brakes, ready to turn around and follow the guy. Without warning the cyclist turned into the Witsoreks' driveway. Hunter, not caring what might happen, followed him.

In seconds both riders were in the clearing. The man rode his bike into an open shed, jumped off it, and disappeared around the carriage house. Before Hunter could go and inspect the green bicycle, he stopped, embarrassed and speechless.

He was not three yards away from Miss Witsorek, who was watering her garden with a hose. She was coming toward him, hose in hand. To run away would be cowardly, so he stood his ground, not knowing whether to expect a cold shower or some hot words. What he got astounded him.

"Oh!" the lady exclaimed, dropping the hose. "It's you! I've been hoping to see you, and explain."

This didn't make any sense to the boy, but she

came up to him and in a low voice told him the story of her younger brother.

Warren Witsorek had spent three years in Viet Nam, twice decorated for bravery. He was captured, suffered horribly, but finally escaped. Back in the U.S., he spent months in a veterans' hospital. This summer he was home for a while. Often he seemed perfectly normal. Other times he thought he was still in Viet Nam, insisted on wearing his army outfit, and was always trying to escape.

Hunter's eyes were stinging, and the lump in his throat made it hard to say, "I'm sorry. I *am* sorry . . ."

Miss Witsorek went on. "I didn't want anyone on the island to know," she said. "But after all, it's nothing to be ashamed of."

"Oh, no! Hunter agreed. "It's like he's been wounded, only worse. I'm sorry I thought he was the bike thief. Is that green one his own?"

The lady nodded. "The same one he had before he went in the service."

Hunter thanked her and then went slowly down the drive, his mind so full of this tragic story that he had rounded Pine Point before he remembered he was looking for Rusty and Jan. He thought about the old dock, with those gaping holes. Maybe Jan had fallen in one and broken her leg. He was getting uneasy about his friends.

At the dock he stopped. To his relief there were no bicycles to be seen. Where had those crazy kids gone? Maybe they had taken the center road home after all, and met trouble. He rode that way, and at the haunted house saw no bikes parked there. He was very tired and still hungry. He longed to go home, eat a big meal, and hit the sack. But he couldn't quit until he found the kids.

At the Cragmore House Mrs. DuPont heard him coming and opened the door.

"Oh!" her voice was full of disappointment. "I hoped it was Jancy."

Hunter couldn't believe his ears. "They haven't showed up yet?" he asked.

"No!" she answered. "Tell me, how can I get help?"

She was so frantic that Hunter suggested he would ride quickly to town and let Mr. Hammergren contact the police.

"Oh yes!" she agreed. "I wouldn't know what to tell them. Just let me know, the minute you learn anything."

It was dusk now. Downtown the street lights were on. Riding past the library Hunter was surprised to see it was dark inside. He was even more astonished to see the cedar waxwing in the front window. That meant a message for him. It had to be about the kids! He tried the door. It was locked. He checked the upstairs windows where Mrs. Purcell lived. No lights there.

Maybe she had left a message on the back door? Hunter hurried around to take a look. Fastened to the door was a piece of paper. He tore it off and ran back to the street light. Unfolding the paper he read:

2:00 P.M. Jancy wants to sketch the haunted house and then we'll go for a swim. Hurry up and join us!

Rusty

They had been gone since early afternoon! How could they have vanished so completely? Hunter's mind was spinning as he hurried to the hotel. Just as he got there he thought of one possibility. The kids might have parked their bikes *behind* the old house. Perhaps Rusty — or Jan — had gone up those rotting stairs and was badly hurt.

As quickly as possible he gave Mr. Hammergren the news.

"How can we get help to them?" Rusty's Dad asked.

"Let's ask Mr. Clemson. He'll know what to do."

Soon they were at the teacher's house. Mr. Clemson took charge quietly.

"You go on, Hunter," he directed. "Tell the kids

155

we're coming. We'll get the police and the doctor, and a bike for Mr. Hammergren. And I'll call Jancy's aunt."

Hunter didn't wait to hear more. Forgetting his fatigue, he raced along the shore road. He remembered stories of people who had been scared out of their wits by ghosts in haunted houses. Of course, he didn't really believe in ghosts, but there was something spooky about the historic house, especially tonight, with the disappearance of his friends.

When he got there he raced around to the back. He was shocked and scared to see that the kids' bicycles were not there. He locked his own and set the kickstand. He felt like shouting, "Rusty! Jancy! Where are you?"

But that was not the Indian way. Instead, he approached the basement door noiselessly, leaned his ear against it and listened with every sense alert. Not a sound. He walked to the porch. Was it only last night he had found the stolen bicycles? It seemed ages ago. He wished for his flashlight but there was no time to go and get it. He peered inside.

It was very dark. He could just see that the ceiling had not caved in, nor the walls. Yet there was a weird feeling of threat, of something wrong. He climbed in, so he could check the stairway. It was just like walking blindfolded. He bumped into a chair, and jumped in fright. Reaching the stairs he crawled up them on hands and knees. Then down again. At least Rusty and Jan hadn't come to grief there.

He sat on the bottom step, chin in hand, trying to think clearly. Maybe the kids hadn't been here at all. Perhaps they tried to come by some other route and got lost in the maze of little used roads. But how could Rusty have stayed lost so long? Another thought slid into his mind. Could their bikes have been stolen?

He felt again the creepiness of this place, and shook his head to get rid of such crazy thoughts. It was then he noticed on the floor a few feet away something dim and white. It reminded him of the white fronts of the old-time soldiers' uniforms. Could the ghost of a wounded soldier be lying there? Was that whiteness moving up and down, breathing? A shiver ran up and down his backbone. What *was* it? He had to find out.

Feeling his way to the spot, he stooped and touched the whiteness with the tip of one finger. It felt like paper, rough paper. A thick pad. Hunter picked it up and carried it to a window. A sketch pad. *Jancy's sketch pad*! It was a solid clue. The kids *had* been here! What a relief!

Then new questions came. Why had Jan dropped her precious pad and left it behind? Had something scared them away? Where should he search for them, now? What could he tell the rescuers when they arrived?

As he stood there wondering, a great-horned owl spoke from the woods. It was like the voice of a friend, telling Hunter he was not alone. He relaxed, and felt better. He cupped his hands over his mouth and echoed the owl's call.

What happened next made Hunter break out in goosebumps. There was an answer to his call, but not from the owl. Far-off strangely muffled tones asked, "Hunnn-tur? Hunnn-tur? Is that you-oo?"

Hunter was shaken by an uncontrollable shiver. It sounded vaguely like Rusty. But Rusty wasn't here.

The voice called again, more urgently.

"Hunter! Hunter!"

This time he realized it was coming from below, from the basement. *Could* it be Rusty?

"Rusty?" he cried. "Rusty! Where are you? Where is Jan?"

"Here! In the basement!" came the answer.

A girl's high voice added, "I'm here too! Hunter — Hunter! Get us out quick!"

Hunter, pushing a chair out of the way so fast it fell over, felt for the edge of the rug and turned it back. His fingers found the trapdoor and pulled the handle.

As the door flopped open he heard Jancy's sigh of relief and Rusty's cheer.

"Come on up!" Hunter yelled into the black hole.

"We can't!" Jan wailed. "Kirby took the ladder away."

Kirby? Kirby had trapped the kids down there?

Hunter's fears melted away. Ghosts were forgotten. Kirby was the thief. There was no more mystery. Now catch him!

All this flashed through the boy's mind as he was groping around for the ladder. Finally he stumbled over it and put it through the trapdoor. Jan and Rusty climbed up and all three rushed to get outdoors. On the porch they paused. Rusty drew a deep breath.

"Wow!" he said. "Now we've got to grab our bikes and go for help!"

Before Hunter could say that help was on the way, Rusty was running around the house, and the others followed. The redhead stopped so abruptly they ran into him.

"Where are our bikes?" Rusty yelped. "Kirby's coming back and we've got to tell the police before he makes his getaway!"

Hunter told him the police were on their way.

"We'd better hide, then," said Rusty. "In case Kirby gets here first. We don't want him to see us."

"You can say that again," Jancy agreed.

Hunter, picking up his bike and leading the way, carried it through the tall grass and weeds to the trees that bordered the battlefield. As they got there Jancy stumbled and cried out, "Ouch!"

Then she began to laugh and couldn't stop. It was her bike and Rusty's she had fallen over.

"Well, I'll be hanged," Rusty commented. "I guess Kirby didn't want anyone to suspect we were in the house, and dumped them here."

"Why didn't he just put them in the basement?" Jan wondered.

Rusty answered that he couldn't do that without giving the two of them a chance to escape. He turned to Hunter.

"You see," he said. "The stolen bikes are in the basement!"

"I know!" Hunter said. "I found them myself last night."

Rusty looked at him in amazement. "You did? How come?"

"I had a hunch, and checked it out." he answered. "How did you find them?"

It was Jancy who answered. "I wanted to sketch the room and the stairway," she reported. "I asked Rusty to shift that rug a few feet. That uncovered the trapdoor."

Rusty took up the tale. "We were excited, opened it, and went down. While we were trying to identify Jan's rental, suddenly the ladder was pulled up, and there stood Kirby glaring at us."

"It was scary!"

Rusty continued, "Kirby said he was taking the bikes off the island tonight, and that we'd have to stay there until he was done. He knew we'd tell people, of course."

"Rusty was cool!" Jancy said. "He told Kirby we'd talk later and he would be arrested. But Kirby said — Rusty, tell how he threatened us!"

"Well, Kirby said that if we *ever* breathed a word about him and the bicycles he would burn your cabin and Indian artifacts. He said he would report you to the police for stealing, and *you* would go to jail."

Again the girl spoke up. "That's when we knew he was bluffing."

There was a pause. Hunter cleared his throat.

"Hold it," he said. "He wasn't bluffing. He found out that I took my teacher's binoculars. But this afternoon I gave them back, so now I can report Kirby, and he can't do me any harm. What happened after that?"

"Well," Rusty said, "When he shut the trapdoor it was so dark I could almost spit out the blackness. We knew there was no way to get out, so we sat on the floor and talked a while."

"Then," Jancy cut in, "Rusty fell asleep and it was AWFUL, alone in that choking blackness. I tried to calm myself by imagining I was walking along the East Bluff road. I tried to picture each house. The third one has a white picket fence. On the gate, in small letters is the occupant's name. Schmitt!"

"*What!*" Rusty couldn't believe it.

"That's right! I knew I had seen the name somewhere! That's not all. I know what he bought the paint for. In the yard there's a doghouse painted red, green, and black! That made me laugh. I felt better, and soon I fell asleep too."

Silence greeted this information. Then Rusty said, "It was the owl call, right here in the house, that woke me up. Man-oh-man, I sure hoped it was you and not just an owl."

Hunter signalled for silence. His keen ears had heard the familiar squeak of the trash dray. The kids watched the shadowy shapes of wagon, team, and driver as they came into view on the road and drove around to the basement door. They heard Kirby's yells of rage when he discovered that his prisoners had escaped. A minute later he was loading bicycles into the wagon in a mad rush.

While he was doing this, the kids heard the throbbing of a powerful motor out on the lake. It got louder. Rusty whispered, "I bet that's his getaway boat!"

The sound came closer and closer before it died away.

"It's stopped at the old dock," Hunter guessed.

If the rescue party didn't show up soon, Kirby would get the bikes on the boat, return the horses and wagon where they belonged, and swear he knew nothing about the whole deal. What proof would there be against him? Hunter knew he must try to keep Kirby at the haunted house until the men came. How he could do that he hadn't the faintest idea.

SABOTAGE

The woods and the darkness hid the three kids from Kirby as he brought bike after bike out and put it in the dray. Hunter was growing more tense each moment. Why didn't the men come? It would be awful if Kirby got away.

"I won't let him!" Hunter said fiercely to himself. His impulse was to rush out there and punch the trashman's jaw. He had been wanting to do that since the blackmailing, but Kirby had muscles of steel from lifting heavy trashcans every day. Perhaps Rusty and he together could knock the guy down and sit on him. Then he remembered Mr. Clemson's warning. He couldn't get Rusty into that kind of danger.

While he was sorting out his thoughts, one of the horses stamped his hoof, making the harness jingle. That simple little sound did it. A plan sprang ready-made into Hunter's head. It was not so risky and it might work.

He whispered his idea to Rusty, who offered to help.

"No," Hunter said, like a commanding officer. "You stay to look after Jancy, in case anything happens to me."

Rusty grunted unhappily, but Hunter paid no attention. He was concentrating on Kirby's moves. The minute the man disappeared into the basement, Hunter stepped out of cover, bent over double. Keeping his eye on the door Hunter moved a few feet. The instant Kirby appeared with another bicycle, the boy dropped to his stomach. Raising his head a few inches he watched the trashman. As soon as Kirby's back was turned, Hunter darted on, and then flattened himself on the ground once more. After repeating this maneuver several times he was close to the dray.

Keeping his body low and making no more sound than a raccoon, he stepped beside the near horse. His fingers felt for the harness, and in slow motion he began undoing one buckle here and another one there. He was glad for the times he had helped his Dad in the stables. If he could detach this horse it would foul things up for Kirby. He himself planned to slip around the house and work his way back to the other two.

But Hunter's luck ran out. Just as he reached the corner of the building Kirby turned and saw him. Leaping toward the boy he grabbed him by the throat and roared,

"What are you doing here?"

Hunter kept his face calm. "I came by, and wondered what was going on," he said.

"Where's the redhead kid?" Kirby demanded in an ugly voice.

Hunter shrugged. "I've been looking for him myself," he answered.

Gradually Kirby's hand let go.

"Well, since you're here you might as well help me. I know *you* will keep your mouth shut!"

He shoved the boy through the basement door. "Get with it, kid!" Kirby said. "You know what I'll do if you don't!"

Hunter, silently whooping with excitement, went in. Here was a chance to delay Kirby still more. He knocked over two bicycles so their pedals and spokes got tangled.

"Clumsy ox!" Kirby said. "Hurry! There's no time to waste."

But wasting time was Hunter's top priority.

At last all the bikes were loaded, and still the rescuers had not come. Kirby put the ladder on top of the load and ordered Hunter to sit beside him. He picked up the reins and gave the team a stinging slap with them. At the same time he shouted, "*Get up*, you lazy brutes!"

Startled, both horses lunged forward. The dray swerved sharply to the left as the righthand horse shot ahead, not pulling the wagon at all. The other horse was thrown off balance and almost fell over.

Kirby leaped to the ground, cursing all horses and harnessmakers. Hunter held his breath. Would the trashman suspect him? Swearing like machine-gun fire, the man backed the free horse into the traces. Hunter let out his breath and jumped down to 'help' him. Kirby made no objection. He failed to notice that as soon as Hunter fastened two pieces of harness together, he separated another set. The boy knew he could never get away with it except for the darkness.

Hunter, with ears straining, thought he heard people coming up the road from Lakeshore Boulevard. To keep the trashman from hearing them, he said, "You sure have been smart, Kirby, engineering this deal. Are you doing it alone?"

Perhaps the praise calmed Kirby. He answered, "You bet! Except for the guy with the boat, and he don't know what it's all about."

At this moment a voice from the road called out,

"Hunter! Hunter! Where are you?"

It was Mr. Clemson and the others. At last!

Kirby, taken by surprise, dropped the strap he was holding and straightened up. Before he could cut and run, Hunter jumped at him, hitting him behind the knees so that he collapsed like a jointed wooden toy. At the same time the boy yelled at the top of his lungs, *"Behind the house! Come quick!"*

Kirby struggled and twisted as Hunter grasped him with both arms and tried to scissor his legs around the man. It was no use. Kirby was much heavier and stronger. He had just broken free when Mr. Clemson grabbed him and jerked him to his feet. A deputy policeman pinned Kirby's arms behind his back.

Hunter stood up, breathing fast, but glowing with satisfaction. At last he had tackled Kirby!

Mr. Hammergren appeared and laid a hand on the boy's shoulder, asking with concern, "Where are Rusty and Jan?"

Hunter's mouth dropped open. He had forgotten about them!

"They're okay," he answered.

Rusty and Jan were already running from the trees, and Mr. Hammergren went to meet them. Hunter started too, but Kirby called out, "Don't let that kid go. He stole the bicycles. I came to take them back."

Mr. Clemson spoke up. "That's a lie, Kirby Tyson. Hunter reported finding the bikes. He told us to come."

"Well," Kirby said with a sneer, "you gotta run him in too. He's a no-count guy, and he's been helping me. Right, kid?"

Hunter felt as though he grew three inches as he answered.

"I made like I was helping," he said, "but I was the one who unharnessed the horse!"

Even in the moonless night he could see the look of hate the trashman shot at him. Kirby tried again. Turning to the teacher he said, "If you don't believe the boy's a crook, Clemson, I'll tell you who stole your binoculars!"

"You don't need to," Mr. Clemson said. "He has returned them."

There was a pause, and Hunter asked, "Whatever took you so long? I thought you'd never get here."

"We wanted the doc to come, in case the kids were injured, and bring us in the ambulance, but he was expecting to deliver a baby any minute, so we waited a while. Then we decided to come ahead on bikes. He'll drive out later unless we send word we don't need him. Thank God we don't!"

While this conversation was going on, the deputy

had snapped handcuffs on Kirby and searched him for weapons. All he found was the padlock and key, which he kept as evidence.

"We've got all the proof we need," the policeman said with great satisfaction, "to get this guy convicted."

Kirby growled. "Except for that blasted boy I'd have gotten away."

"So it was Hunter who delayed you!" the deputy said. "Tim, aren't you proud of your son?"

Surprised, Hunter looked around. "Is Dad here?"

"He was," Mr. Clemson said. "We met him as we were leaving town, and he came along. I wonder where he got to?"

"Oh!" said Mr. Hammergren. "I forgot to tell you. Just as we left the shore road, he told me he heard a boat near by. He went to check it out."

Rusty spoke up. "Hey! That's the boat to pick up the bikes. Do you think Hunter's dad will capture the guy who's running it?"

"He'll sure give it a try," the deputy said, "but he may need help. I've got to drive the dray and Kirby back to town. Will you two men," looking at Mr. Clemson and Rusty's dad, "go down to the old dock and see what's going on?"

Mr. Hammergren said he thought he ought to get

back to town as fast as possible to let Mrs. DuPont know Jancy was all right.

"I'll take care of that," the deputy told him. "I've got to send word to the doctor, too."

Unclipping his walkie-talkie he sent the messages. Then he put Kirby in the dray, securing his feet with a cord. He clucked to the horses and drove off.

The kids brought their bicycles from the woods, and with the two men rode downhill toward the lake. As they turned onto the shore road Hunter urged complete silence. When they were near the dock they laid down their bikes and walked.

At the end of the dock Hunter saw the outline of a good sized fishing boat. No lights showed, but the motor was idling. A whiff of cigarette smoke, the kind his Dad used, drifted to his nose. On the dock near the boat he could just make out a strange lumpy shape.

Making the kids wait, Hunter led the men carefully over the treacherous planking. They found Tim Martineau sitting on a man who wore a yachting cap.

"Please!" the man begged. "Get this giant off me, will you?"

"What happened?" Mr. Clemson asked.

The man explained. "I was waiting for a friend, and this guy as big as a grizzly bear jumped on me and had me down before I even knew he was here."

In the darkness Hunter grinned. So Dad hadn't for-gotten the skills learned as a boy from Grandfather!

"It's okay, Tim, you can let him up now," the teacher said.

Tim and the boatman stood up and stretched. From his height of six-foot-four, the man looked down at Tim and shook his head in disbelief.

Mr. Clemson asked why he was there. He said he had come to pick up some junk Kirby Tyson was going to re-cycle.

"Re-cycle!" Mr. Hammergren exclaimed. "That's a good joke! That 'junk' was a cargo of stolen bicycles. Kirby is on his way to jail."

The boatman was shocked. "You mean — I'm in-volved in a crime?" he asked.

"Looks like it," Mr. Clemson said. "Unless you can prove you didn't know what Kirby was up to."

"I'll be a witness for you," Hunter spoke up. "Kirby told me you didn't know what he was doing."

"That should help you," Mr. Clemson said to the man. "But you'll have to come along with us. Will you take us in your boat, or walk while we cycle?"

The boatman chose the easier way. Soon the people and their bikes were on board. He revved up the motor and the boat swung slowly out into the dark lake.

The three men moved toward the bow, to talk

with the boatman. The kids sat in the stern, on cushioned lockers.

Suddenly the redhead poked Hunter. "Bet you can't guess who went with us to the Soo Locks yesterday!"

"Okay, tell me."

"The man with the built-up shoe!"

"You're kidding!" Hunter said.

"*Really?*" Jancy asked.

Rusty laughed. "He's an inventor. He's staying at Island House, and tries out, on different kinds of bikes, his inventions to make bike riding easier for people with all kinds of handicaps."

Hunter sighed, and shook his head.

"I bet you can't guess what I did yesterday!" Jan challenged them. "I called on Miss Witsorek!"

The boys looked at her in amazement.

"What happened?" Hunter demanded.

"She was working in her garden and let me drink out of the hose! I asked her if she got lonely way out there, and she said no, she had her father and brother. Then she asked about *me!* I told her about riding around with you two, and how much you needed to solve the mystery of the bicycles."

"Man-oh-man!" Rusty exclaimed. "You've got guts! What did she say?"

"She was quiet for a minute. Then she said, 'Oh. Is

one of them a tall, black-haired youth?' I said yes, and that you are a grandson of the Old Chief who just died. Then her phone rang and she went to answer it, and I started home. I didn't discover anything, but I liked her!"

"Wow!" was all Rusty could say.

"Jancy," Hunter said thoughtfully. "You did more than you know. Today when I followed that same guy in there again, she was ready to talk to me about him. He's her brother, a hero. Wounded and a prisoner in Viet Nam. He's not really well yet. I told her I was sorry, and she understood. Without your help, Jan, we would never have uncovered this part of the mystery. Thanks."

By this time the boat had circled the west side of Mackinac and was approaching the harbor. Suddenly Rusty remembered something else.

"Hunter!" he exclaimed. "*Did* you have a dream? What happened?"

Very briefly Hunter told about Walking Buffalo, and taking the binocs back to Mr. Clemson. "Right after that," he concluded. "We heard that you two were missing, and I've been on your trail ever since."

They were almost at the dock, and the men rejoined the kids. Tim sat down beside Hunter, laying a big hand on the boy's knee.

"How about coming home with me, son?" he

asked. "Instead of riding back to the cabin? Your sleeping bag's already there. Remember?"

"It's a deal," Hunter said.

"Great!" said Rusty as they all climbed off the boat. You'll be on the spot to see what happens tomorrow morning when people find out Kirby is the thief!"

"And I will escort Jancy home to Cragmore House," Mr. Clemson volunteered.

"See you tomorrow!" the kids called to each other as they went their different ways.

THE TRAIL AHEAD

That night Hunter's last thoughts before he fell asleep were about the reward money. He would get fifty dollars for finding the stolen bicycles. Too bad he and Rusty couldn't have captured Kirby too.

By morning the whole village, the whole island, buzzed with excitement. The mystery of the disappearing bicycles was solved! Kirby was a villain, and Hunter a hero. The story grew like a snowball as it passed from person to person.

Neighbors crowded around the Martineau house, eager to hear all about it. Rusty came too, full of news from downtown. Hunter was glad to have his help answering questions. Later on they were surprised when Jim Redding, the mimic, knocked on the door. Rusty let him in, and Jim went straight to Hunter, who was embarrassed, not knowing what to say to this island celebrity. Strangely, Jim seemed at a loss for words too. At last he said,

"Hunter, that was a dirty trick Kirby and I played on you. I'm danged ashamed, and sorry."

"Trick?" Hunter repeated, puzzled.

"You know," Jim went on. "That tape with the siren and 'the Old Chief's voice'. I thought it was a joke. Now I realize Kirby was afraid to have you living so close to his hideout."

"So that was it!" Rusty exclaimed. "But how did he play the tape in the night?"

"It was attached to a timer, and hidden in the woodpile," Redding explained.

"And that's what he had in his paper bag the next day!" Hunter said. "I'm glad to know. Thanks, Jim for telling us."

Redding apologized again, and left.

Not long after that, the telephone rang. It was Mrs. Purcell asking Hunter and Rusty to come down to the library right away. Hopping on their bikes, they took off at top speed.

Outside the library Hunter was surprised to see a whole group of people — Jancy and her aunt, Mr.

Hammergren, Mr. Clemson, *and* Tim Martineau, as well as Mrs. Purcell. What was going on?

Jancy, on tiptoe with excitement, called out, "Here he comes! Hunter the Hero!"

The others laughed and cheered. Tim was beaming with pride. Hunter couldn't say a word.

When they had all crowded into the little building, Tim asked Mr. Clemson to tell everyone the good news. With a smile the teacher said,

"As we all know, the island needs a new trash collector, starting today. The mayor has offered the job to Tim. Tim will do it if he can have Hunter as a paid assistant for the rest of the summer. The mayor can give Hunter a 'limited work permit'. When the tourists are gone and school starts, Tim feels he can handle the job alone. What do you say, Hunter?"

Hunter thought quickly. It was outdoor work, and regular pay. He would get to know his Dad better. And Dad would be earning money the year round!

"It's great!" the boy burst out. "Super!"

Tim put his hand on Hunter's shoulder with a smile that reached into his dark eyes.

"Hooray!" Rusty shouted. "Martineau and Martineau, Collectors to the Island!"

Everyone laughed, and then Mrs. DuPont stepped forward.

"Hunter," she said. "Yesterday you rescued my

niece from a very nasty situation. To show my appreciation I will get a pair of excellent binoculars for you, because you are going to be an ornithologist. I—"

Scowling, Tim interrupted her. "Ma'am, my boy will collect trash, but I don't like for you to call him names."

"Tim!" the teacher said quickly before anyone could laugh. "The lady is giving Hunter a very honored title!"

"Oh, sorry." Tim said, with a nod toward Mrs. DuPont.

Mr. Clemson went on. "There's one more important piece of business." He took an envelope from his pocket, handing it to Tim's son. "Hunter, Mr. Piperman, speaking for all the rental bike owners, asked me to give you this, with their thanks and congratulations."

Hunter's heart sank when he saw the thin envelope. He had been thinking about a thick wad of bills. Without a flicker of expression he said, "Thank you."

Slipping his fingers inside the envelope he drew out a single bill. It didn't look right. Then he glanced at the number on the corners and gasped in astonishment. It was a one-hundred-dollar bill. The first he had ever seen.

As soon as he could speak, Hunter said, "But it was the policeman who arrested Kirby."

"Well," Mr. Hammergren told him. "You were the one who made the arrest possible and easy. Everybody agrees on that!"

When the excitement had cooled down, Tim and Mr. Clemson took Hunter into the little office.

"Son," Tim said. "You have done well. If you want to stay on in the cabin this fall, it's okay with me."

Hunter glowed. He wouldn't have to move! Chief Walking Buffalo was right. If you put your feet on the right path, things go right. Suddenly, surprisingly, he felt unsure. It *was* lonely in the cabin without Grandfather. It would be worse in winter. Yet, living in a crowded house in the village still seemed unbearable.

"I — I don't know what I want to do," he admitted.

"Would you like to stay with me during the school months?" Mr. Clemson asked.

Hunter thought he was joking, but the teacher's face was serious.

"You can be free as a breeze — for bird study and all that," he said, "as long as you keep your grades up."

Hunter couldn't take it in. "Are you really asking me to live in your house? Why?"

Looking him straight in the eye Mr. Clemson answered. "Because I believe, with the right educa-

180

tion, you can be one of the first Native American ornithologists. Does that appeal to you?"

"You know it!" Hunter said. Taking a glimpse into the future, he saw the trash job. Other jobs. College! He could become a real Bird Man.

"Well?" his Dad asked. "What do you say?"

Hunter had one question. "Can I bring the Indian treasures to your house with me?"

"Of course," came the teacher's answer.

"Thanks, Mr. Clemson. I'd like that. And I promise you won't be sorry."

Beaming, the three went out to the main room where Mrs. Purcell was serving juice and cookies.

"To celebrate!" she said.

Hunter took his two pals off to a corner to tell them his latest news.

"That's swell!" Rusty said.

Jancy was very thoughtful. "You know, Hunter, I can hardly believe it. All the weird things have suddenly fallen into place, like the missing pieces in a jigsaw puzzle. It's terrif'!"

With a wide smile, Hunter nodded. Then Tim called out,

"Son! We need to harness our team to the dray, and get started on our job!"

"Hey!" Rusty cried in dismay. "Then I won't see you again. Dad and I leave on the two o'clock ferry!"

"I'll be there to see you off!" Jancy said.

"So will I," said Hunter. "I'm sure Dad and I can work that out."

When the time came, Tim stayed with the dray on Main Street, while Hunter ran to the ferry dock. In a minute Jan rode up, and she and Hunter were talking about her aunt's gift when the Hammergrens arrived with their bags. Goodbyes were said all around.

Soon the ferryboat sounded its mournful toot. People crowded on board, and everyone was waving.

"Come again!" Hunter called as the water widened between boat and dock.

"I will!" Rusty yelled back. "And you come to Minneapolis!"

Hunter raised his arm in Indian salute. Rusty and Jancy did the same. It was a promise.

SOURCES

I. The author's experiences, photographs, and notes made during five years spent on the island (1960–1965) and on later visits.

II. *Supplementary Bibliography*

Birds of North America, by Robbins, Bruun, Zim, Singer

A Field Guide to the Birds, by Roger Tory Peterson

Famous Indians, by U.S. Dept. of Interior, Bureau of Indian Affairs, 1974

Historic Guidebook, by Mackinac Island State Park Commission

Indian History is a Study in Change, Minneapolis Star, September 8, 1969

Indian Life in the Upper Great Lakes, by George I. Quimby

The Loon Feather, by Iola Fuller

Lore of the Great Turtle, by D. Gringhuis

Mackinac Island — Its History in Pictures, by Eugene T. Peterson

Mystery of the Gulls, by Phyllis Whitney

The Patriot Chief, by Alvin M. Josephy, Jr.

Retrospect of Western Travel, by Harriet Martineau, 1836

Straits of Mackinac! by William Rattigan